CALASADE

SANGUINEM ISLE

COPYRIGHT

DEDICATION

To the love of my life.

Without her, nothing would contain worth.

Not even writing.

AUTHOR'S NOTE

Calasade is a Greco-Roman world. Because of this its mother tongue is Latin, so you will find within Latin words and terms. Note that some liberty has been taken with a few of these Latin instances to make its consumption easier and more consistent for those unfamiliar with the language.

PRODITIO

His sides cramped and red-hot iron scalded the inside of his chest. Worse, his knees kept buckling, hindering the desperate attempt to flee his would-be killer. Not just any spider scurried after him—oh no, not here in this place so infamous for its butchery people named it Silva de Clades, the forest of carnage. Few foreigners—which he was—possessing a rational mind dared tread anywhere within Avia, homeland of a gray-skinned people called Saeva, but especially *not* within this woodland.

To do so was to tempt the god of fate and get sentenced to the awful, eternal nothingness of Afterdeath.

If only he could reach the cabin where safety waited to meet with him in the form of three Saevorum warriors. Ironic and tragic he had gotten within sight of the cabin moss-enshrouded and leaning to the right, visible between leaf-heavy, dipping branches.

In opening his mouth to shout, he gasped a hoarse whisper.

And ran-limped ever onward while fighting the urge to glance over his shoulder. The arachnid, big as any horse and too heavy to sprint, darted in short bursts on eight hairy legs, any of which were suitable for spearing him. Fangs as long as his forearm oozed venom that brought paralysis in a few heartbeats, giving the araneum plenty of time to spin a cocoon. Not the way a man wanted life to end, entrapped in a silk prison and pitching uncontrollable fits as the poison did its job of turning his lips black and skin pasty, liquefying his flesh and enabling the araneum to suck out his meat.

What honor did such a passing hold?

By the sounds the spider made he might have assumed a quartet of heavy-footed people gave chase. That was how aranea ran, similar to a handful of folk stampeding on wood, except one of them lurched.

Thack...thack-thack-thack. Thack...thack-thack-thack.

The monster was too close. No outrunning it. A hard life, the weight of his broad-axe, and a bad ankle broken years ago were too much to overcome. He heard the *clack-clack-clack* of fangs and ducked, rolled, rested on bended knees.

The spider blurred past and went from sight though not hearing. Much too close were the snapping of twigs and breaking of foliage.

He kissed the honed head of his axe, entreating the god of fate for mercy and wishing he fought from the start to avoid confessing cowardice that Fatum might deem as a reason to bar him from blissful Afterlife. The entreaty finished—sure these were his final moments—he thought of his wife safe in their house and tried to utter, "Me love you" in her Saevi dialect. They were the three words of her language he had bothered to learn because they formed the lone sentence he believed mattered.

Until now.

Had he learned to bellow help, he might live.

Or possessed the air to scream.

The forest fell quiet. No birds chirping. No giant spider scuttling. Just his wheezing. He inched to his left to peek around a shrub, squinting from the sweat stinging his eyes. Were it not for overwhelming terror, he might have found the wherewithal to take one hand off his broad-axe—a mistake gripping the weapon so tight, he knew that, but was helpless to do otherwise—and wipe at the perspiration. He pled for clearer vision, then wished the plea had gone ignored.

Six saucer-sized eyes lined in a row and shining as emeralds trained on him from a head sprouting ash-colored, wiry hair. Fangs glistening in watery liquid clacked against each other.

Slow.

A little quicker.

Fast.

Much faster.

Oh, Fatum, your benevolence please.

The araneum rushed at startling speed. He leaned, willed his trembling hands to draw back the axe.

Wait.

Wait...

He swung too soon. The axe missed the spider's body, striking instead a spindly leg. Were the gods righteous this day, the crack his axe made meant the blade had hampered the araneum. He rolled in the direction the spider had come and scrambled to his feet. With his weapon raised high, he roared; his posture and ferocity worked well for frightening bears. Whether the feign was effective against arenea—

Thack...

Fatum.

...thack...thack-thack...

Mercy. Show mercy.

—Clack-clack-clack.

Sidestepping, faltering, he swung. His axe ricocheted off the teardrop-shaped abdomen black and shelly. An aranei leg knocked him to the ground, its serrated edge slicing through his vest and nicking his side.

Too late he regained his feet. The araneum crashed into and sent him airborne. When he landed, the araneum loomed atop him. It was then he found the air to scream long and loud. Using his last bits of strength, he took hold of the fangs stabbing at him and pushed with the success of shoving a rooted tree. Venom dropped from the fangs' tips to blister his face. This time his scream matched that of a woman in full-terror. The scream cost him his focus, vitality. His arms quivered. The fangs got nearer, ever nearer, and pricked him. Did his cheek sizzle or was that his imagination? The pain was real—oh yes, the pain that seared along his jawbone akin to someone taking a red-hot poker and dragging it across his face.

He shrieked, shrieked until his throat went raw and urine hot and wet flooded his groin as he pissed himself.

Soft whistles and whirring filled the air.

Thunk.

Thunk.

Thunk-thunk-thunk.

The araneum stumbled off, wavered, scurried a few feet, and dropped. Arrows poking out its head quivered. In breathing a sigh of relief, the would-be victim closed his eyes and thanked Fatum for Saevorum help. When he looked, he saw a leather-clad gray-skin warrior peering back, eyelids shut to slits, an angular face painted in purple tribal tattoos smiling.

"Pray-da-toor," said the Saevum.

Praedator took the hand offered, smiling his relief over being saved but also at the way Saeva mispronounced the nickname his wife had given him. Even she could not say it proper since Saevorum dialect was as their nature—violent and abrupt—their tongues unable to produce the lyrical syllables common in Praedator's patois.

He nodded to the other two warriors before taking a step and faltering. Was that the aranei poison working or his nerves making him feeble as a babe? His eyesight was clear, his sweating due to the temperature, but his wanting to throw up...No, this was not the poison. Nerves. Had he any piss left, he reckoned to still be wetting his trousers. He waved for assistance and got it by way of a Saevum on either side lifting him under the armpits. They carried him to the cabin with the effort it took to haul an amphora of wine. Impressive and frightening, how they lugged his large frame, their physical prowess underscoring the verity they could snap his neck as easy as their claw-like thumbs and forefingers.

Inside the cabin—a single-room wherein the source of light was gaps in the shoddy roof—the air breathed stuffy. His palms clammy, Praedator rubbed his hands together and sneezed before perching on a barrel. The Saeva sat on the other side of a table, warped, atop which was a singular object. A middle Saevum nodded at the wax tablet. Praedator picked it up, studied the sketches scratched into the wax.

The first drawing portrayed a herd of beasts known as bimembrae; ferocious animals bipedal and cunning, muscular bodies hairless. Despite their bone-crushing strength, the creatures' claws and protruding jowls ranked as their chief threats. Next to the bimembrae a stick-figure held up items appearing to be a staff and a whip. The figure represented a magum bestiae, one trained in the art of controlling beasts via thought. Beneath the stick-figure and herd he counted forty squiggled lines under an encircled "C". These symbolized gold—chrysae—wages for a beast-master. At least he hoped his guesses correct. So frustrating, the inability to ask. If his wife had accompanied him...

Why had she not? He recalled the spider. Obvious that.

Praedator shook his head, returning himself to the now, and contemplated the coin, the drawings. He wondered why Saeva needed a beast-master. The obvious reason was they lacked any magical ability. Just one of their kind throughout their long history had proven capable of anything stronger than witchcraft. For generations they had gotten along fine, so why the sudden need for...?

War.

Yes, war had to be the reason. They wanted to amass an army of bimembrae and to do that they needed someone from Praedator's race. Did they intend to hire? He turned the word over and over in his mind. No, the three warriors across from him— their nation —would never risk engaging a foreigner who might tell on their plans or take their money and fail at the job on purpose, not when the past shared by Regna and Saeva was hostile and untrusting. To Praedator's knowledge he counted as the solitary Regnum allowed inside Avia and he certainly cast no spells.

He looked at the trio across from him, raised his eyebrows, and shrugged.

"Ewe bees plageearus," muttered a Saevum.

Ewe bees plageearus? He kept resounding the words in his head until he got what the middle warrior had tried to say.

You be plagiarius.

Beads of sweat reformed on Praedator's forehead. The coins were to be his for *kidnapping* a magum bestiae—a disagreeable act even if possible. Bloodlines had been diluted. Power weakened. Sacred practices abandoned. Certain gods forgotten lost capacity, faded into obscurity. The conjuring the greatest Regnorum magae now managed was utilizing whatever elements might be in proximity. Rocks hurled and earth parted. Fire controlled. Breezes enhanced to gale-strength. Water set from a lake or river. Formidable these magum elementa but rarer per every generation that further distanced his race from its forebears. Scarcest of all was the magum omnipotens able to summon magic from nothing.

Chills replaced his sweat as he realized that thanks to his wife, Saeva were aware of these Regnorum matters and more. Praedator had met her on a hunt. He should not have been in Avia or gotten past Bestialis's Wall, the fortification she patrolled that day which alienated her Saevi state from his own. Nor should he have survived their encounter. Her country's law bound her to kill trespassers, but a heat of a different sort ensued during their fight and that had saved him. Attraction led to love and love to marriage. Lucky he, unlucky couple they; each barred in the other's homeland. Weeks went by without them being together. One day—during a bright and sunny, glorious afternoon he marked as the best day of his life—she informed him her government had awarded him citizenship. He should have asked how she managed the miraculous feat of convincing them to do so. Much later the realization dawned she reported everything of note that had passed his lips and now, as he sat here examining this tablet, he wondered whether her love was real or a masquerade to keep him talking.

Magum bestiae. Bimembrae. Echoes of terrible times when Regna battled Saeva in a war eons ago that left Calasade scarred to this day. He uttered a phrase the warriors could understand. "Great Confrontation?"

They nodded.

Praedator gulped to settle a bout of nausea. Regna had won the Great Confrontation through the power of their magic-laden ancestors long deceased. In their absence Regna would struggle to win any renewed conflict. Praedator scratched his bearded chin and pondered the havoc war manufactured, how it ravaged a land and ingested populaces.

Which was worse if he and his wife tried for neutrality?

If Saeva lost, her limbs might get nailed to X-shaped planks and she displayed at the side of the imperial highway as proof of Regnorum superiority. Whereas if his people were beaten, he could find himself clinging to life and begging for death as his body slid along a pole embedded in the ground after it was shoved up his natis. The third option of aiding Saeva and becoming a traitor had a possible, brighter outcome.

Those forty bars of chrysae were enough fortune to last a lifetime or three, get him and his wife far away across Mali Sea. All he had to do was kidnap someone. Not a big ordeal, not after he reached the heart of parallelism where kidnapping measured short standing next to treason. Not such an impossible task either, were the job given preparation. To be sure traipsing Calasade's countryside searching for a victim was foolhardy, but if he thought about it, considered it in earnest, he might come up with someone from the myriad of places he had stayed in his travels. Near amphitheatrae presenting bestial entertainment maybe.

And there he had her—the slave living at a previous employer's villa, a young woman of beauty silly and naïve. Her brother's failure to inherit their father's beast-master talent had caused her family to fall into servitude. She being the daughter of a man who believed women inferior was probably never tested.

Praedator put his elbows on the table and brought together his fingertips. He mulled the trout confronted with a stream dividing into two. How did the trout know which rivulet new to him ended in a waterfall and which fed a pond littered with tasty flies?

Every decision, when you got to the heart of things, came down to blind chance.

II

IMPERATORI

Tempus Turbulentorum, a.CDXCIX

The alcoholic halted in front of colonnaded spaces overrun with produce stalls, ragged slaves, and shoppers haggling for lower prices from toga-wearing purveyors. With spring upon them, the people—most of whom he detested—tended their business with renewed vitality, bickering loud and endless. Across the street of concrete overlaying stone loomed his nemesis, the Twisted Vine, a two-story tavern twice wider than tall, its limestone walls painted the color of purity, the terracotta rooftop looking ablaze in light of the downing sun. Three arched windows spanned the Vine's upper floor and another two separated by a vast doorway were on the ground level. Shadows lent the front a mysterious, come-hither quality that caused his gut to hollow until butterflies took flight.

In life preceding sobriety he had often frequented the tabernum, but since quitting the drink, he had tried to eschew the Vine. For the good it did. Regardless his efforts of pluckiness he nevertheless fell vulnerable to circumstance, as now, though usually he could blame the Vine's heady temptations. The place was an ever-wily seductress tugging at his elbow and murmuring in his ear, an alluring she-devil who insisted he submerse in the gaiety of her customers and partake of her gratifying whores. Aromas that might have been the most damning of temptresses enticed through fruity wine and the yeasty perfume of fresh-brewed hops. His breaths drew shallower as he reminisced about how the brew's bitter tanginess lasted long after swallowing. He closed his hands into fists, their surfaces scarred and bruised, his palms calloused. Their current condition was poorer than when he last squeezed dice while playing poker and feared losing, the exhilaration building prior to his last-ditch effort of capturing victory and gaining salvation.

He snorted with disgust at his cowardice. What *man* feared his own soul or a straightforward duty? He just had to go in, get the coin, and come out. Children with a penchant for misbehaving managed an errand so simple.

I shall not wager—

He rubbed his palms together to erase their clamminess...

—nor will I—

...and wiped his lips.

—drink.

Lightheaded to the extent his body seemed to float, he shrugged his shoulders to feel the reassuring weight of the swords sheathed in their back-harness. Those blades were iron, albeit rusty—their material thus what he must become. He took a deep breath before trudging across the street, his legs inflexible as stilts, back akin to a plank.

A guard confusable for a bear due to his breadth and furry clothing blocked the Vine's entrance, a large paw extended to receive the phallic knucklebone that confirmed his membership.

He reached into his pouch and brought out the piece of wood he had handled during desperate hours he would have killed for a drink. Midway to giving Bear Doorman the knucklebone, he pulled it back and ran his thumb over the dates of issuance and expiration. He rubbed the whittled-out letter 'V' hovering over a circle. The two together symbolized a vagina and anus, fitting because the Vine was as famous for its prostitutes as it was its drinks. He turned over the knucklebone. Printed on this side was a sequence of letters undecipherable to anyone except those employed at the Vine. He remembered how the man who had written the code smiled in a sardonic way when asked what the letters meant. That was—oh, longer than he cared to admit, a time affluent and happier when the price did not matter. But it did.

Always does.

In the end his desire for drink and entertainment had cost a lot more than that small fortune.

"Are you handing it over," asked Bear Doorman, "or will you to continue to fondle it like you do your cock?"

"Here."

Bear Doorman studied the nonsensical writing. "Your name and the amount you paid."

"Caderyn Fortis," he answered. "Three thousand gold coins."

Bear Doorman returned the knucklebone and waved Caderyn onward to a wending hallway. Frescos limning sexual acts covered the walls and ceiling. At a second doorway a second guard challenged his right to be there.

Certified a final time, Caderyn crossed the threshold into a theatre-sized room containing squared tables and a grand fireplace. Seated gamblers and conversers were serene islands set in the decadent undulation of naked prostitutes herding customers paying a hundred silver to upper-story rooms. For the patrons compensating fifty, the transaction got consummated in whatever spot proved convenient. The deals, though expensive compared to the prices of lesser establishments, were a bargain. Lupae here were attractive and cared for by the city's finest physicians, advertised to be free of lice and disease.

He went around a woman bent over a table and the lupum spearing her from behind, then almost tripped over a redhead whose thighs squeezed the waist of a man mounting her. The woman's moans were still audible upon Caderyn's nearing the brick-adorned bar that stood midway to the back and offered free food stored within bowls. Vegetables, fruits, various meats. He pushed his way through the bar-crowd busy ogling the sexual festivities he had passed and others including men sucking one another's cocks and women fondling each other.

The barman filling a clay chalice was of slight build. Stringy tresses hung on either side of an aquiline countenance that showed distaste after he gave the calix of wine to a customer and looked at Caderyn. "Aio?"

Caderyn gritted his teeth. "Aqua."

"An odd request," the pincernus replied, "for the patrons here never remain sober. Or is it you are already intoxicated? Nulla, your eyne are clear, cheeks unflushed. Will an ale mug suffice?"

"Cleaned of alcohol's taint."

The pincernus fetched a mug from a shelf and dipped it in the bar's closest water-well. Caderyn hoped it was not the same used for cleaning dishes. No, that was the other on the far side, the well with soap residue sticking to the rim.

"You," the pincernus declared, "are at the wrong place for avoiding past demons."

"Yet I am to meet one. A tall fiend carrying a broad-axe. He has a bulbous nose, messy beard, carrot-colored hair past his shoulders. Also limps."

"You describe the hunter of beasts."

"Acteon is present?"

"Of a sort. Are you Caderyn Fortis?"

He nodded.

"I was ordered to watch for you." The pincernus gestured at a corner set aglow from hanging oil lamps. A bald man in a beige toga sat at a table and was busy arranging circular pieces on a game-board sectioned off by squares. "Proconsul Lepidus paid me naught to introduce you. If you want to meet him, do it on your own. Me, I have more important duties than coddling a stingy nobilis and a..."

Tuning out the barman, Caderyn sipped his water. Acteon had never mentioned a third party—strange considering any territorial governor was noteworthy, especially one willing to come in a beast-hunter's stead given venatores were regarded just higher than reprobates fighting in arenas. An ill-omen but worse was the proconsul setting up a game called Imperatori. Caderyn's favorite, it was an expensive strategy game that got into the blood of those harboring intelligence and the penchant for taking risks.

"Pincernus." Caderyn ran a hand through his hair then scrubbed his forehead.

"Aio."

"What is your fee to inform the proconsul I prefer to talk here?"

"A copper coin."

Caderyn withdrew an aes from his pouch and flipped it to the pincernus who nodded and went. Lepidus looked up and to the side. The proconsul's head shook before tilting towards the game-board.

The pincernus returned. "You must join him."

"Did he say why?"

"Do you take me for your clucking hen? Ask the proconsul...or not. I care neither way. In fact, what I care for least is you. Look at you dirty and ripe, a former public servant dismissed for dereliction of duty now no better than a gutter-dog begging for scraps in the streets you once policed."

Frustration at watching others swilling and enjoying drink when he could have not a single sip; that was sickening enough without having this snooty slave talk down to him. The two combined was too much. "Be careful, *servus*."

"I may be servi, but I am servus *sublimis*. Should you dislike how I talk, take up the issue with my dominus. Let him laugh in your presence rather than your absence as he oft does. He says you call yourself a big adventurer. Hah, in his eyne and mine, you will forever be the braying ass that forfeited his entitlement through drink and games."

"You miserable...!" Caderyn slapped the insolent bastard then yanked a knife free of its belt-sheath.

Patrons eager to see if the pincernus invited Death hushed while the bartender continued to gaze, indignation lurking in his eyes that ticked to the side—a sign guards had probably come up from behind Caderyn.

The sharp tip pricking Caderyn's back was confirmation of that. A grave voice warned, "Do not die for so little an affront."

That threat's underlying sincerity and the too-familiar shame over losing control of his emotions triggered Caderyn to stow his weapon and hang his head. Dice rolled across tabletops. The guards behind him retreated. The elitist pincernus shuffled to his station. Folk chuckled. He heard snickering and someone declaring, "Bah, same new Caderyn unlike the old. A drunk to-day and a hero yester-day. Still thinks he is the former, though in truth he is naught but wind. Full of bluster and little else."

Maybe after getting the coin he would stay, empty his filled pouch, drink and pass out, drink again when he awoke, drink and drink some more, forget what he was, the nightmare that had happened, and the man he had been, drink until he stopped caring enough to postpone forsaking those who loved him and—

"Fortis," a man shouted. "I am Proconsul Lepidus and I wish to share words. *Come.*"

The man sitting in the corner waving had grown accustomed to giving commands; his sharp intonation forbade disobedience. Once Caderyn arrived at the table, the proconsul picked up a satchel and dropped it onto a stool. The satchel jingled.

"Acteon," said Lepidus, "sends his regards."

Caderyn eyed the money owed, thinking if the coin belonged to Lepidus, the proconsul would demand an exchange he could ill-afford. Better, he decided, to learn of this Lepidus before taking the man's purse. "From where do you hail?"

"Permia," answered the proconsul. "Regio Bordia to be exacter."

"A considerable journey. What brings you this afar south?"

"Sit." Lepidus stroked the game-board, his finger tracing the outer edges. "Let us converse and compete as civilized men are wont to doing."

Caderyn gulped, kept his mouth closed. To speak at that instant was to expose a shaky voice, such was his longing for holding Imperatori's round pieces of ebony and ivory.

Lepidus cocked an eyebrow. "That satchel I dropped onto the stool contains over two thousand gold coins. You can afford to gamble a few paltry chrysae while hearing a proposition that could change your life."

"I..."

"A moment. That is what I require in trade for satisfying the debt Acteon owes you."

He sat an arm's length from the table. "Expect me to listen but not play."

The proconsul's eyebrow arched higher. "Verum, you wish to forgo a game? You ogle Imperatori as a forlorn lover might the woman gone from his embrace for a decade."

"It has not been so long."

"Three years then?"

Caderyn briefly closed his eyes. "How much has Acteon told you?"

"Enough." Lepidus picked up a white game-piece. He set the marker on its side and flicked. The piece spun, slowed, wobbled...toppled. "Nine years ago we in Bordia started construction on an amphitheatrum the world has heretofore never seen. Our inaugural games will feature the best fighters from throughout Calasade competing in a group fight with no quarter given. The remaining survivor of this coetus bellum shall want for naught."

"What has that to do with me?"

"I am a proconsul up for reelection after the inaugural games and owner of a ludus. It behooves me to fill my stables with the highest quality stock."

"Stock? Do you see cattle upon peering across this table?"

"Neither cow nor pig or horse. I see a man lashed by his own whip."

Insults knew no bounds to-night. "Yet what I am is a former soldier, afterwards an exquisitor for this city of Polus, and now a sword-for-hire. None of that includes being an harenarius. You have sought the wrong person."

"I disagree. In my mind men brave enough to have fought on a battlefield can be remade into ones who fight on the Bleeding Grounds. Acteon said if I needed a true warrior, you were it. He also said the three years that construction should take for us to complete the Bleeding Grounds will be enough for you to train. I would have you leave here at my side."

"Side?" Caderyn laughed. "You no more consider me your equal than I deem the pincernus worthy of sucking my cock."

"Have it your way. You shall leave here yelping at the end of my leash."

He scratched his palm, considered the knife at his hip. "I am no servus."

Lepidus sneered. "We who want something are servae regardless our station. A Rector answers to the makers of law, the Lex Latum, and to his or her senate, the Superum. The Lex Latum and Superum—indeed, all politicians—serve the people and lobbyists. A wife obeys her husband and the husband her; children their instructors, parents, siblings, and friends. You, Caderyn, kneel to those of loftier station and anyone hiring you. Your master changes per the task you accept, aio, but if subsisting is your goal, you shall *forever* have a domini."

"Everyone must make a living unless" —the proconsul tapped the Imperatori board— "you gamble and win. A satisfied man uninhibited by necessity is the only real freedman."

Caderyn leaned forward and took a game-piece, recalled amphitheatri festivities that had not happened in a decade since games outside executions and killing animals were outlawed until this year. People who enjoyed such barbarism were nothing more than sycophants romancing Mors, the god of death. "What of the coin?"

Lepidus's smile revealed teeth white and straight. The man was a liar, a servant to nobody. "I have had my moment. The coin was Acteon's. Now it is yours."

"Irrespective of my reply?"

"Aio."

Caderyn let loose of the game-piece and stood. He took up the satchel, wincing at the din of a band playing a lewd tune, mugs slamming and dishes banging to the song's tempo, feet clomping, drunks singing, the lupae shrilling laughter. Along with the overwhelming noise came a sea of expressions ranging from sad to blank to happy to rapturous; arms held overhead, hands clapping or shaking dice, whores caressing their tits then someone else, giving sidelong stares, a bite of the lip here, a nibble of the earlobe there; people dancing, fucking, voyeurs salivating. Wine's fruity scent and the root-like odor of brew were there and gone, masked in the stench of perspiration.

Someone squeezed his wrist. He looked down to find the proconsul's cheeks flushing, gray eyes steeling. Caderyn shook his arm free. "Insist I join your plight and see your hairless head severed."

The proconsul's face paled. "My intent was to bait you. Spring is coming. Visit, see Bordia. Mayhap you will change your mind upon witnessing the new arena. One never knows."

Caderyn waited for the throbbing in his temples to wane. "Realize the day will never dawn when I step foot onto your Bleeding Grounds or anyone else's. How many are being built across Calasade? Ten? Twenty? Each is an insult to the sanctity of life. That said, apologies for my temper. The environment—*this* tabernum—tests my resolve to keep the oath I gave my wife."

"You mentioned working as a sword-for-hire, yet did not elaborate as to the tasks you undertake."

"Mercenary work, protection, safeguarding valuables. Things of that nature."

"I see." Lepidus waved him off, the. gesture obvious in underscoring who between them was master and servile. "A pleasure to meet you."

"Likewise," he lied and walked towards the exit. He stopped to look back upon reaching the threshold at the hallway, saw Lepidus reclining against the wall and staring upward. The proconsul did not react to the pincernus bumping his knee.

The sourness in Caderyn's mouth worsened. A politician so withdrawn in his schemes he failed to chastise a slave's clumsiness was a snake in the garden.

III

HORRIFICUM

Wearing naught—

—teeth chattering—

—trapped in a pit—

—staring at the moon that never seemed to move—

—cowering.

Weeping.

Growls from outside rose in pitch and bordered on the screams of a person getting tortured. The beasts making those spine-chilling noises stood upright on powerful hind legs, their bodies brown, hairless, gargantuan, heads horned. She saw the caged monsters after her captors whisked her off a ship and up a mountainous incline but before they lowered her into this earth-prison, its mouth a mixed symbol of freedom and blinding fear because she could do nothing to protect herself should a creature break loose and leap inside with her. The beast's fangs would shred her, its claws flay her.

Maybe, she reasoned, her captors intended for her to be food.

The mere thought forced her to squat, as if doing so might provide safety, as she boggled for the umpteenth time over why anyone captured such monstrosities and delivered them to this island.

Located where?

Wood snapped from up top. She held her breath and clawed dirt, hoeing rows and praying a gray-skin was not coming to fetch her. Everything about these strange people, apparent partners of those scum that had stolen her away, screamed brutality—from how the gray-skins spoke in a choppy and angry manner to how they moved, how they *laughed*.

She shivered and retreated until rocky points stuck her shoulder-blades. How she wished for home, her brother, mother, and father, Lepidus's villa, the orchards, her quarters, bed, the companionship of servae and the guards patrolling the grounds. Caratos was friendly, sometimes a little too flirtatious for the proconsul's liking. She missed his humor, missed all of it, but she especially missed her clothes. Strange how the clothing's warmth had gone unappreciated, but there then the weather rated tepid, good for sniffing citrusy-smelling shrubs or eating cherries that exploded in your mouth as you bit into them, the temperatures quite unlike here, deep in the ground where the nippy air ponged of brine and sunrays rarely shone. In daytime, arm-rubbing chilly while at night...

To stop her teeth from chattering, she jammed her fingers in her mouth and yanked them away, having forgotten for a moment their filthiness.

For how long had the ship that carried her here sailed? When did they take her? There was a...a what? She groaned from the strain of pushing through a thickening fugue, from the stabbing sensations at her temples.

What happened the night her captors, the plagiariae, came?

There had been a...She reheard the proconsul's nasal voice invite her to dinner. Her nerves running amok, she said yes, but even if she wanted to decline, no slave dared deny their master. Lepidus then led her to a linen-covered table. His hand cupping her elbow comforted her and contained a hint of...

She could not summon the word, but did recall the tingling his touch sparked.

Private that table. Seats for two. Candlelight. Fresh flowers in a vase. Pork minced and marinated with herbs, pepper, and nuts. "Dormice," comprised Lepidus's lone-word reply to her inquiring the dish's name. Succulent. Rose-flavored wine to complement the dormice.

There followed pleasant conversation. He asked of her childhood, the home she lived in before joining his house, of her brother, mother, and father. She could tell his empathy over being apart from them was sincere because of the sadness with which he spoke and how his eyes softened.

He got up at that point, excusing himself and going to fetch a present.

His gift to her.

Comely the nightgown. Saffron print. Thin, inappropriate, titillating. He instructed her to try on the clothing, so she took the nightgown to her quarters and donned it, relishing how the silk brushed her skin. She laid on her bed and gazed at the birds painted on her bedchamber's wall. Pretty, mystifying robins. In the wavering lantern-light those birds flew an illusionary flight. The birds dimmed, blurred. She was falling asleep and did not want to; Lepidus would come. A proconsul's interest in her, a low plebs since her familia defaulted on debts, was flattering. His intelligence fascinated her—she always the fool for smart men—and perchance the nightgown indicated he wanted someone to replace the wife nipping at his heels.

Wrong, this wanting a married man—her parents raised her to respect such institutions—but in being presented with a slim chance of gaining freedom, she found scruples to be irritating flies puff-shooed away.

She imagined Lepidus's embrace. His kisses. Caresses. Her eyelids closed and she drifted off, dreamt of better days and pleasurable nights until the dreams turned into the nightmare reality of a cloth getting stuffed into her mouth and reeking of an offensive balm applied to wounds. The man shoving the rag between her teeth looked through lifeless eyes set wide apart in a scarred face that brought a primal sort of fear she had never known.

His face went fuzzy, faded as she grew woozy and weak, her shriek never passing the pungent cloth. Unconsciousness came, wore off later as someone lugged her across Floridus's port. There stood Judoc, the dock operarius, directing her abductor to a ship.

Scarface cursed her wakefulness and covered her mouth and nose with the rag, pressing his fingers into her gums through her cheeks.

Blackness resumed.

How many hours until she re-awoke naked, chained spread-eagle to a table? Waves crashed against the ship's hull. Portal light. Not enough to see. Just enough to prick. A nondescript form hovered over her. Familiar, the cut of the man's shoulders, that scar...

Scarface lifted a jug.

Foul-smelling water splashed into her mouth and flooded her throat, causing her to swallow even as she retched. Cloudiness swept into her mind. She suffered dizziness, stronger nausea, lethargy, and longer periods of unconsciousness. Whenever Scarface brought more of what he declared medicine, she clamped her jaw shut. Her chin smarted still from the many times he forced the metallic-tasting swill down her gullet.

Awful memories not the worst. The worst hinted at why her thighs were tender and genitals stung. She wished—did she truly?—nulla, premature wishing for the kiss of Mors, not unless

Death kissed her during sleep and she was unable to experience hurt or trepidation—had become weary of both—but she could not rest.

What if during her sleep...what if...?

Beyond the pit's mouth emerged conical trees intermittently blocking parapets that crumbled in places and led to a demolished gate. The ancient fortress granted some shelter. Why did her captors dwell in the open subject to rain and wind and—

So much...remained...unknown and...She shook her head, hard, uncaring of the throbbing where her head hit after she fell on one of her escape attempts. Anything to stay awake. Not the hour for rest, past time to prepare for a gray-skin or plagiarius coming for her. She scoured the pit for something to use. Rocks that might serve as bludgeons and jutted from her prison's walls and the ground stayed affixed. Her knowing this did not keep her from scratching and tugging and cursing and pleading while trying to extricate them. The rocks proved as unmoved by her desperation as her captors when she begged the plagiariae to set her free and they guffawed at her.

How heartless did a person have to be to dismiss her wailing in so callous a manner? Who were they? What had they done and what did they want with her, a serva?

How, who, what, what.

She wished for an end to her unrelenting questions, but the thing she most wished for was her father and how pater coddled her after she hurt herself playing as he trained the...What her kidnappers wanted came to her like a zigzagged bolt illuminating the sky. No choice; she had to get out, flee, told herself it did not matter the pit measured several times her height or that her knees threatened to buckle, told herself neither was it of consequence her legs wobbled in getting her to the wall with the most outcroppings. She climbed, whimpering each time her fingers gripped the jagged rocks, moaning when those edges cut into the soles of her feet.

The pain was unimportant. Nothing compared to what her captors planned.

Halfway up she found no more rocks to use. She searched the flat piece of wall and reached for a root slimy and wet. Her weak grip slipped. For a moment she thought she might fall and felt her burgeoning hope shrivel; a grape left out in the sun.

Nulla.

This was the farthest she had ever gotten and she refused to stop now. Sobbing, she gripped harder, cried from the cramp in her forearm. She pulled. Lifted. Her feet left the rock-footholds. Her arm trembled, almost quit as her chin came level with the root and the root started cracking.

She closed her eyes, begged for that root not to break, but it did. She plummeted along the side of the pit, the rocks now traitorous weapons that jarred and bruised and scraped. Like a cat, she clawed, trying to get a handhold, leaving her fingernails behind and palms mangled. Her falling seemed to be a never-ending nightmare, but when her feet hit the ground, the real horror began. She lay there prone on the dirt, sand, and rocks, her mouth gaping open and bringing in just enough air to keep her alive while she stared at a night-sky and listened to someone screaming as a beast roared.

IV

PORCUS

The pig strung up earlier that day to bleed-out weighed too much for the butcher's aged trusses and now laid among busted timber. This was to Caderyn's benefit. He had been walking the alley when the framework crumbled and offered to perform the jobs of rebuilding the trusses and skinning the pig. Because he never before skinned an animal, he explained to the proprietor, he volunteered a reduced rate. Said butcher detailed how to skin and sent him after lumber. That errand ate up the majority of the morning. His excavating the broken-off frames from the holes took the rest.

Around mid-afternoon the heat reached its zenith and his body ached for rest. He finished replacing the two Y-frames spread ten paces apart by working the second support into the hole like the first. Next came filling in the holes and flattening the dirt. The beam to rest horizontal on the Y-frames for dangling livestock caused his knees to wobble. Unable to lift that high enough to fit the beam into the Y-frames or even over his head without breaking his spine, he dropped the piece of lumber and went to the shed where he had gotten a saw, hammer, and nails. A rope thick and strong lay coiled on a top shelf.

He fashioned the rope around the beam then threw the rope over a branch of an oak tree. The makeshift pulley-system allowed him to hoist the beam, albeit still with considerable effort, where it dangled above but did not align with the Y-frames. His yanking the rope using several short tugs got the beam positioned and he let the beam drop. A loud crack preceded the Y-frames swaying. He held his breath, fearing his labor for naught.

At last Fortune befriended him. Those frames held.

A ladder got him high enough for untying the rope and running it through a new pulley on the underside of the beam. The subsequent item on his to-do list was raising the sow to strip its hair. Before that, however, a second wind; he sauntered under the oak to take advantage of the shade and trained an eye on the butcher shop's rear window—its proprietor had made adamant his disapproval of any respite—until a shadow fell upon the windowsill.

While grousing and wandering over to the hearth, Caderyn reminded himself he was lucky the butcher hired a hand. He knelt to pump the bellows and get a fire going—fitting since an inferno might as well have consumed Acteon's coin courtesy of Lepidus. Months of overdue rent, other debts, compensating men who joined him on the previous contract for which he had gotten jilted, food, weapons and armor the smith judged as unsalvageable. New was expensive, also wasteful as things turned out; near three months without an offer for any kind of decent paying work. Summer was ending, the profitable season thus ending and leaving him facing a dismal winter of hunger unless he stumbled across enough menial jobs. An embarrassing thing scrounging for pitiful amounts of coin, but blistered hands and a bruised ego were better than starvation.

That, anyway, was what he kept telling himself.

He shoved the bellow's handles together. Air whooshing out the flame-scarred nozzle turned the embers an angry red. Several more compressions got the embers to ignite and flames to dance. He gave an additional squeeze for good measure then rose and gazed down at the big pot that his arms barely encompassed when hauling it from the shed. The pot's water lay still at first, bubbled, commenced to boiling. He stuffed a wool blanket into the pot using a stick and stirred, staying on the alert for the tiniest splash because water like that blistered skin.

Similar to this damnable weather.

Caderyn leaned the stick against the hearth and wiped sweat off his brow. More waiting done in the shade crouching behind the oak, hidden from prying eyes that might spy through the window.

Leaves of trees covering the rolling hills beyond the alley fluttered in a breeze too weak for cooling this back-alley. Across from him—stained by blood and shit and piss from the butcher's stock and by ale and wine that had lopped out amphorae—was a warehouse that a pack of filthy dogs used as protection from the sun. The dogs alternated their stares from the pig to him and back to the pig. Perhaps they pondered whether they could outrace him to the tasty treat or on how much meat they could gorge prior to him chasing them off. He clutched a rock and heaved it at the pack, just missing a brown and black salivating retch. The rock's colliding with the wall discharged a brownish plume. What mutts did not continue staring licked themselves.

"Mangy curs," Caderyn grumbled, rising, his knees popping and joining in on the complaints his back issued.

Awakening come the morn would be groan-inducing.

He limped over to the workbench to grab a pair of meat-hooks. Those he jabbed in the pig's hind ankles, affixed a chain to them, and tied the rope dangling from the pulley to the chain. After walking under the beam and knotting the end of the rope for getting a better hold, he faced away from the pig and plowed ahead. The rope bit into his shoulder and put pressure on the small of his back where a knot formed; still, he made progress. At least until his feet slipped. His heels digging in, Caderyn lumbered forth struggling to breathe and wishing he could close his mouth to stop it from leaking saliva his body needed, the real-life frustration as high as what he suffered during those dreams in which he fled and got nowhere.

The barking mutts wagged their tails. Maybe they celebrated his reaching the long spike driven deep into the ground or they laughed however dogs did as he practically lost his hold trying to secure the rope to the spike's eye.

Back at the workbench among knives of various sizes and shapes was a scraper the length of his forearm, its serrated and dulled edge curving in the middle. He took that along with a pair of pincers for retrieving the blanket. The butcher said a hot blanket draped over the pig eased scraping hair off the sow, so Caderyn patted the blanket as instructed, scalding his palms and rattling off a string of curses that startled the dogs.

Stupid curs.

Too restless for partaking of the shade, he paced and willed time to go by faster, forgetting how long the butcher said to wait before scraping. To ask was to get reprimanded—the butcher had made his hatred for repeating himself plain, too—so Caderyn kept marching, staring at the cracked grout in the road and remaining unaware of wiping his lips until they bled. The wiping was habitual; what he did when the urge to drink was strongest and all he could think about was drunkenness's euphoria and how winning at Imperatori embellished his elation.

Three years.

Three long insufferable years.

Spent in a wasteland of want.

Caderyn again paced under a cloudless sky and merciless sun, now in front of the Twisted Vine. Sweat—from the temperature, his day's labor, the jaunt home to retrieve every coin he possessed, the journey here—drenched him. Passersby in this affluent part of the city circled wide of him either due to his stench or because sane people possessed an innate desire to avoid the unhinged.

Drink, drink, drink.

That edgy mantra supplied the tempo to his headlong trips back and forth along the Vine's front. He begged for sterner will, an inspiring recollection, a bolt of lightning—anything to suppress his madness. The only thing that came was a mind's eye picture of his wife. Elianna's mouth warped in sexy innocence, her laughter effortless and intoxicating leading up to her kissing him, her body flush against his.

His stomping increased. Fists formed harder rocks. He remembered the tears she spilled after he informed her he wagered and lost their villa, that they were forbidden to take any furnishings and no longer owned horses for riding or a veranda for dining or private baths for lounging and cleaning. No more nights lazing in a bed stuffed with feathers or eves walking in a garden she cultivated for years, a garden which somehow filled the hole within her that their inability to have children created.

She cried quietly, never raising her voice to him while her tears ran faster and she entered the hovel he rented saying, "Ashes of the past, my husband, are that from which true worth rises."

She had articulated those words to fortify him in their darkest moment. What she should have done was believe his proclamation he was unworthy of her, that she should stop hanging onto a man blinded to his own selfishness. Why had she not realized there was rot within him that caused him to seek his own downfall and would bring hers?

Some battles were unwinnable. The war taught him that.

At the Vine's entrance, Bear Doorman requested Caderyn's knucklebone and snickered as Caderyn held one shaking hand with the other.

"Check the symbol," Caderyn spat, "and send me along."

"Anxious are we?"

"Te pedicabo." He seized the phallic knucklebone and shouldered his way past the guard to whom he just said fuck you.

In daytime the doorway at the end of the frescoed hall was unguarded, the room beyond serener, most tables unoccupied. Of the five where people sat, three were taken by lupae giving him expectant glances that changed to morbid curiosity. Was his imminent self-destruction so obvious? Others avoided looking at him altogether. The exception was a blonde woman, her hair cut in the short style of a man's save for the bangs draping her forehead.

She smiled.

A fellow romancer of gloom.

Caderyn gave her a nod and turned to his right. Nuts, fruits, meats, and vegetables sat in tiny bowls on the U-shaped bar. The same pincernus was cleaning, drying, and shelving mugs. He let go of the towel and dipped a mug into the well.

"Not aqua," Caderyn told him.

"Nulla? Have your chickens roosted then?"

"I—"

"Eleison, say no more! Let me serve *you* by deducing what you want. It is, after all, the function I crave to perform." The pincernus poured out the water and stroked his chin. "Before me stands a muscular oaf tough and dirty head-to-foot. Wild tresses, shit-colored and mingling with what appears to be porci hair. Unshaven, cleft chin. Hmm, a bent nose. That and the scar on his cheek indicate he has received his fair share of lumps. Not severe enough, though, for he yet insults me and the fine people present with each breath he takes."

Caderyn lunged forward and slammed into the bar.

The pincernus retreated out of reach. "Your palms are blistered and in far worse shape than your clothes. Those are new, aio, but sweat-stained as your padded brown breeches and vest. That shirt is old." The bartender pointed above Caderyn's shoulder, just to the side of his head. "Those mucrones you carry in your chest harness must have been freshly forged. The bulbs of their hilts are unblemished, gold plate." He twirled his forefinger. "Turn for me."

"I think not."

"Very well. *Custodes!*" Three guards wielding spears and shields marched from the backroom behind the stairs. "Relieve this man of his weaponry." When they had, the pincernus gloated. "My seeing the weapons and their scabbards are unimportant. I know what you favor."

"Enough of this," Caderyn growled. "Return my swords."

"Gather them upon exiting. As for your chosen drink, it is not nectar of the gods. Vinum is too refined for your sandy tongue. You who led men into battle and were later responsible for investigating crimes are the worst type of reprobate. *You* are a nobilis turned barbarus and *barbarae—*"

"Are needed." Freckles peppered the blonde woman, her irises jade, nose narrow at the bridge and little wider at the bulb. She yet smiled through thin lips. "I am Jana of House Lepidus. For a fortnight, each day and well into every eve, I have lingered in this cesspool because no one could tell me where to find you."

He cleared his throat, shifted from one foot to the other. "What is it you want?"

"Not here." She tipped her head towards an arched window. "Outside."

He reached for the beer the pincernus placed on the bar.

The woman grabbed his wrist. "Later. You have a task to perform."

"What task?"

"Come." She moved away from him and spun around at the threshold of the hallway. "Stay rooted then and know your refusal shall cost a woman her life. Know as well you forfeit a fortune unless you gather your swords *this instant* and follow me."

V

CONCORDIA

The café's snow-white, woolen awning brought a welcome relief from the sun. Caderyn pulled out a chair for Jana then sat facing her at a table adjacent to an outside granite bar inlaid with diamond-shaped marble. A waiter arrived to inform them the Thermopolium de Calasade served hot, tepid, and cellared refreshments. Today's specialty was the delicate Jasmine East, tea available for a limited time seeing as how orchards in a mysterious land across turbulent seas harvested the mint-flavored leaves every five years. The waiter scribbled on a wax tablet after Jana shook her head and requested a concoction of herbs, wine, and orange juice called aranciata.

Caderyn found her drink as distasteful as his peppermint-spiced water. He scraped his tongue along his front teeth, thinking that bore more flavor than drinking the menstratum et aqua that lacked a brown-yellow tint and sediment promising texture.

He turned his gaze on Jana as the waiter left. "What is this regarding?"

"I will get to it in a moment," she said, tilting her head and staring. "Proconsul Lepidus neglected to disclose much about you. He did, however, mention one worrisome thing. How extreme is your thirst for drink?"

With a grimace and shaking hand, he raised the goblet and sipped. Worse than imagined. He put down the goblet hard enough to splash its contents. "Are my tremors too subtle?"

"Apologies if I offended you. My curiosity got the better of me. I wanted to learn..."

The way she was watching him hinted at morbid curiosity. Could be he might have greater minded the sensation of getting poked and prodded if not for her eyes and—

"...your affliction?"

He peered downward. "Apologies. You asked me something."

"Aio. What it is to battle your compulsion."

In the early stages, before want had escalated to desire, a headache thumped at his temples. As his need blossomed the thumping expanded across his forehead. In the center of that was a penetrating nail. At that lovely juncture he suffered sweats hot and cold. It was then that trivialities sent him into a blind state of rage wherein he succumbed to or survived the storm, aware that should he outlast the tempest and find peace, the peace was momentary and the tempest's return inevitable.

A sigh came from Jana.

So, too, did one exit Caderyn. They had just met. Irrespective how dazzling her irises or impatient she, he was unprepared to share intimacies. "I have difficulty putting the experience into words."

"I see." She tapped the tabletop with a painted fingernail before leaning forward to put her crossed arms on the table. Branded skin peeked out between the edge of her black glove and tunic's beige sleeve.

Caderyn drained his goblet. "Are you a serva?"

"I was. Once." She removed the glove and rolled her sleeve to reveal an L-shaped mark above her wrist. "My husband—*previous* husband—accumulated debts I repaid."

"Why you and not he?"

"A body making restitution from the grave is most difficult."

When their gazes locked, shivers coursed along his spine. Caderyn looked off to the people in the market street; the masters wearing togas and their slaves donning rags. A few of the toga-wearers barked for their slaves to hurry filling carts. Elianna and he had met among those hawker stands. She a merchant's daughter, he the conscripted recruit. The perfume she had worn—a small intake of breath made him aware of a honey scent. Thinking the sweet alyssum a memory-smell, he realized it came from Jana and tilted away. "Who is this woman you mentioned at the Vine, the one whose life you claim depends on me?"

Jana's crow's feet deepened as she squinted. "Indrasena. We remain ignorant to who took her and where they ferried her."

"And the proconsul asked for me?" He frowned, shook his head. "Someone intimate with the area and its people is a wiser choice to learn those things and rescue her."

"The proconsul has faith in you for reasons unknown to me. I tried convincing him otherwise, but" —she shrugged— "as are most adorable men, he is a stubborn boy in need of an occasional swift kick to the natis." She swirled the aranciata with her index finger, then inched the finger into her mouth.

"Could be," he reasoned aloud, helpless not to watch her suck, "Lepidus fears a local exquisitor is vulnerable to coercion. How important is Indrasena to him?"

A pop coincided with Jana sliding out her finger. "Fifty thousand chrysae."

"That is...a hefty sum." He resisted clearing his throat. If he had gotten naught else from the years of gambling, at least he had become privy to his own giveaway signs. "Is she a relative of Lepidus?"

"I am limited to discussing immediate details and bartering your fee."

Barter? Fifty thousand chrysae then was the starting point. Caderyn fought hard to control his burgeoning grin and conceal his wish that the price escalated enough he could escape the rot of his life, purchase land for farming or ranching, whatever got him miles outside temptation's reach. "Tell me what happened."

"She vanished in the middle of the night. We were unaware of her missing until the next morning when she did not show up for breakfast. Once the proconsul's hysterics ended, we searched the villa and its immediate grounds. We discovered a ladder on the atrium's roof next to the opening where rainwater falls through and suspected the slaves in the house. Then, when they appeared innocent, we questioned those tending the orchards. To no avail."

"Why do you believe she lives?"

"We found no indications of violence. I assume were murder the intent..." She ground her teeth. "Perhaps I am mistaken. This uncertainty may well drive me mad."

He nodded, commiserating. "Sometimes, Jana, knowing is worse. The reality becomes a nightmare and the nightmare inescapable." The speed with which her head shot up told him he had said too much. Unfortunate the years of gambling had not taught him to think before talking. "Where did Indrasena sleep?"

"Quarters accessing the atrium. Prettier than most with its robin-decorated wall."

"Was it always painted thus?"

"Nulla. A private chamber and art were gifts from Lepidus upon acquiring—her arrival."

Lepidus doting on her hinted she was no slave. So, too, did her having quarters. Servae slept on the floors of their master's home...which raised a strong likelihood that the kidnapper knew where Indrasena slept and possessed knowledge of Lepidus's home; otherwise he or she would have rummaged and awoken someone. That the kidnapper was a friend of Lepidus or member of the proconsul's familia was unmentionable without proof. "Lepidus lives in a typical villa?"

"He does."

Caderyn pictured the rectangular layout, where the vulnerable points of entry lay. "A novice plagiarium sneaks in via the garden at the villa's rear. There the walls can be scaled and a ceiling is nonexistent. On the other hand, an experienced criminal takes into consideration a peristylium is fraught with planters and tools. Disadvantageous in the dark."

She tipped her goblet. "When spotting you I deemed you a simpleminded brute. I am glad to learn a brain lies beneath that unruly hair."

"Mayhap we should tip our drinks to the misleading nature of initial impressions." A ghost of a smile got the better of his poker-face. "At first glance I thought you scandalous."

"And now? Am I viewed as virtuous? Have I become a forbidden delicacy all-the-sweeter?"

Magic existed in her returning his burgeoning grin with a teasing half one, how its effect made the squeaks coming from a cart's wheels take on a hollow, ethereal quality. Everything grew distant, like the world was retracting. Caderyn shifted in his chair. What had he last, was he—yes, pondering entry-points. "Did you search Indrasena's room?"

Jana's eyebrows furrowed. She finished her aranciata and summoned the waiter to place another order.

"Jana—"

Her extended forefinger interrupted him. When the waiter had gone, she muttered, "Semen was on the floor of Indrasena's closet."

"She is how old?"

"Young, not long past womanhood. No signs of struggle, so—
"

"The plagiarius gratified himself while hiding in waiting?" Crass and vile that, the man awaiting Indrasena to fall asleep in such a manner so he could nab her, the surprise affording her little opportunity to retaliate or cry for help. But what would the kidnapper have done afterwards? To sneak through additional rooms in exiting the house and dragging a girl unconscious or struggling was too risky. "At least one accomplice must have helped him in escaping, mayhap by pulling the pair up through the atrium's compluvium where you found the ladder. Did you discover a rope?"

Jana shook her head.

"How low is the roof?"

"Close enough to the ground for jumping from or lowering a bound person."

"Any suggestions regarding why she was taken?"

"None."

"Describe her relationship with the proconsul." A personal attachment was a fine basis for demanding a high ransom.

"That is beyond what I can discuss."

He said, "Hum" to avoid voicing his frustration. "Mayhap other reasons besides coin or politics fueled Indrasena's kidnapping. Is she beautiful?"

"You judge that," Jana rattled off, sounding agitated, "upon seeing a painting of the—her."

Artwork done in the woman's likeness; inarguable she greater than a slave. "I have not agreed to come."

"Lepidus assumed you assenting is a forgone conclusion."

"Has he? Such hubris given I already declined an offer of his."

This time when she tilted her head, the light in her jade irises was softer and relayed childlike inquisitiveness—rather endearing. "The proconsul bases his reasoning on an event in your past. I am unsure what. He only said that whatever happened was unspeakable."

Again, Caderyn smelled sweet alyssum. Now from memory.

"Caderyn," Jana said, her pitch mounting, voice screeching a little, "there is no time to waste considering. Indrasena disappeared a ten-day *prior* to my arrival in Polus. I need an answer."

He hoped his noncommittal shrug appeared genuine. "Bordia is a long way, the travel arduous, those perpetrators foul. I wager—*guess*—the challenges are formidable."

She frowned. "Shall you not even attempt to help?"

"Due to great expenses the least I will take is sixty-five thousand chrysae."

"That price is too high. Bordia is afar, verum, but Lepidus lives in the port-city Floridus. We can ride horses east from here for three days to Dahak and board the merchant ship responsible for my passage to your" —she sniffed— "*fine* city. After setting sail, we will arrive in Floridus within eight days, eleven should winds be against us. The entire trip ought to take a single fortnight or less and cost you naught. Fifty-seven thousand."

"I wish to bring people who can help me hurdle whatever obstacles may arise and they will require pay."

"Why bring a party?"

"We will need steal Indrasena back should those responsible for her kidnapping not want a ransom or Lepidus refuses to give one."

"How many men do you plan bringing?"

"A thief who is also a capable fighter, a fellow ex-soldier, and a healer. I must factor their wages along with the costs of food, board, weapons and armor. Sixty-eight thousand."

Her laugh hinged on sardonic with an undercurrent of amusement. She cocked her head to the other side. "My father—Fatum kiss him—always told me that when the well nears drying, you ration the water. I can procure the horses and act as your healer. You and your *two* partners will stay at Lepidus's villa. Free room and board. Sixty-*three*."

"Sixty-*five*."

Her cheeks went aglow in pink. "Sixty-two."

"Five."

The stare they shared deepened in the subsequent silence and the air seemed to thicken. She reached across the table, her open hand stopping midway.

He almost took it.

"Sixty-three," she whispered. "We can make up the difference through other means."

"Such as?"

Her tone dropped another notch. "A night with me."

"That much for us to fututio?" He snickered. "You must be a sensational ride."

A blush starting at the base of Jana's neck painted her freckled face. "Is my proposal so ludicrous? Or do you find me heinous?"

Heinous? He found her gorgeous and wanted to say just that, but it was safer to keep his opinion a secret. "Even if the sum were reasonable, I am married."

She swept her gaze to the table. "Apologies. Sixty-five then."

He opened his mouth, stumbled over what to ask—from where she originally hailed, what type of death had befallen her husband, did she have children, why work for Lepidus, and was it he who had been her master. Maybe, Caderyn reconsidered, it was foolish to learn personal details. Knowledge was sometimes dangerous. Reflecting on how his heart had beat when she reached for him, he realized so could she be.

"Shall we" —he coughed— "leave the day after the morrow? I will need time—"

"Whatever you require."

"—to gather my men. The, uh, our meeting place to depart. Here? Dawn?"

"Aio."

"Very—until then." He rose too fast and knocked over his chair. With a blush, he started his journey home.

Late that night Caderyn tried sleeping in a prone position, but raucous merriments in the city—*what did they celebrate?*—traveled the handful of miles to his hovel, sounding as if the festivities occurred at his doorstep. He rolled onto his side and slung an arm over his ear. The frame dug into his ribs, so he flopped onto his stomach and breathed in the stale mattress. Once more he lay on his back.

Him having the chance to rescue this Indrasena and secure a future despairing as early as this afternoon, he should have been happy, sleeping as the dead instead of suffering constant thoughts of Elianna and having new worries surface.

Lepidus requesting his aid so soon after their first meeting was a bad omen, similar to the undiminishing image of the proconsul sitting at his table in the Vine and paying no heed to the pincernus bumping him. Jana's inability to say anything of note equally troubled. Why had Lepidus limited his messenger's ability to supply information that could prove crucial? Somewhere in Indrasena's history hid the motive for her getting taken, feasibly the identities of her kidnappers.

He slipped into a fitful slumber, dreaming of a freckled face, green eyes, rosy lips, a lithe neck, his caressing perky breasts, teasing erect nipples, of sliding his tongue along Jana's stomach and between her thighs to—He jolted awake, heart hammering, and glared upward into the darkness, set on ignoring his pulsating erection.

Lonesome hours passed before sleep revisited and he dreamt of a forest, that he walked a trail wending around shrubs looking sedentary, but if he ventured too close, the bushes sprang and stuck him with thorns. Farther on where the bushes lost the ability to harm they grew larger and in greater abundance, creating a natural oven in which breathing was arduous. The desire to flee filled him yet remained weaker than the emotional pull calling him forth into a clearing. There he rested, if just for a brief spell and prepare for ...

For what did he search?

Puzzled, he strode across a plush field, hairy wheat tickling his palms as they brushed over plant-kernels. Here the sun hung in an untarnished sky and imparted a sense of freedom. The light brought warmth and the revelation he had come to request that the wooden man point the way where death held no sway.

Several hundred strides delivered Caderyn to a weathered spot and the exposed roots of an ancient aspen. Dark nubs on the tree's bark formed eyes, nostrils, and a mouth. Two gnarled, leafless branches grew in either direction.

Licking his lips hurt. Had he been wiping them? "Aye...lie...een...nee." His sandy tongue had murdered his wife's name.

What did he do when thirsty?

Drink.

A mug materialized in his hand. Violets—Elianna's favorite vini spice—seasoned the wine inside it. He worked up some saliva and spoke clear. The aspen shook. Its bark glimmered and released a periwinkle hue that expanded into a large shimmering plane, its ripples surging and erasing the aspen. In the tree's place stood a cave's craggy entrance.

Something rotten in there. He inched closed and sniffed, gagged, willed himself to run.

Like the tree, his toes had taken root.

From the dark depths of the cave Elianna spoke in a pouting voice.

Want not another, my husband. Come. Within. I am buried. Within. Rescue...me.

He stepped forward. Chill sank into his core. Inside the cave his exhales clouded his view of the mist hissing out jagged pores and fogging the floor, though not fast enough to hide the headless skeleton half-buried in a layer of mud. No sooner had he whispered a breathless command of "Violenter tollitis libero" to wake the dead than cobalt sparks burst throughout the haze in brilliant zigzag patterns.

Thunder echoed. Fog parted.

A skull covered in matted tresses rose through a divide in the cave's flooring. Thin lines of blood trickled from the matted blonde hairline and skirted his wife's eye-sockets. Inside those twin chasms moved the split ends of forked tongues.

Serpents!

He awoke to someone weeping. Him. It was him.

Sleep was now hopeless; no point in laying there. The bedposts complained, rusty nails squeaking, to his sitting up and draping his legs over the bed's side. A fire crackling drew him to the window. Bonfires burned in the distance. He had forgotten last night that commemorations occurred to honor the conflict waged between Fors and Permia. Today there was a parade scheduled in which organizers wished him to participate. Caderyn had declined because the man awarded honors for his leadership was dead in spirit.

He retreated from the window and went to a rickety stand, feel-searching to locate the flint and steel. Upon finding the char-cloth as well, he struck the flint against the steel until the cloth smoldered and a flame sparked. To the flame he put the candle's wick and the candle in a holder.

Candlelight did nothing towards making his single-roomed shack and its disjointed walls cozy. A fire-pit for meals and a source of heat in winter had been dug in the middle of what passed for a kitchen. Off to his left were the bed and several crates. Some contained old garb he could never bring himself to wear while others overran with Elianna's clothing. A chest at the foot of the bed held his padded breeches, vest, and a shirt. He donned them, a pair of bracers, the chest harness and its twin swords, afterwards affixing his coin pouch to his belt.

Ashes of the past.

It was time, yes, past time to depart and leave no bridge for returning. Caderyn heaped several crates of clothing near the fire-pit. The twigs and dried grass he gathered he stuffed among the fire-pit's charred logs and lit using the candle's flame.

"Ashes of the past," he mumbled, "are that from which true worth rises."

VI

CLEPTUS

Pedestrians walked the road connecting the empire's three states and those states' major cities alongside drawn wagons and carts. Caderyn joined those eastbound disappearing into the yellow-orange dawn flaring off Via Calasade. The trip from what had been his hut normally took an hour and his sense of smell went unoffended, but not on this day given the congested traffic and the livestock depositing piles of manure. Miles onward the highway thinned and led upward, the ramp's city-walls measuring many times taller than the herd of travelers squeezing people elbow-to-elbow on their way to the tunnel-gate Porta Septentrio. Caderyn inched forward beside a toga-draped old man leaning on a walking cane. The old man's wife, whose over-sized shawl mostly concealed her summer dress, hobbled on Caderyn's left and utilized him for support.

Their halting owed itself to guards deeming a merchant suspect and spending several minutes inspecting the merchant's wagon while horses neighed, oxen stamped, and folk grumbled their displeasure about waiting in the humidity and the gods knew what else. Likely none of them were readier to get moving than Caderyn. It had been months since he last saw the men he wanted to bring and now worried either had accepted other assignments or be gone for the day by the time he reached their homes, assuming he survived this stench causing him to pinch his nostrils and glare with envy at the old woman who held a perfumed cloth to her nose.

She looked at him, eyebrows arched, the expression knocking off ten years of age except for the area of her forehead. There wrinkles had deepened to creases and reminded him of the trails snakes left in sand. He realized she had asked something, but never got the chance to discover what; the custodes bellowed for the line to get going and go they did, pushing and shoving Caderyn and the old couple inside the tunnel lasting a hundred-odd strides. He came out on the other end blinking, his eyes now unaccustomed to brightness.

His turn off Polus's main thoroughfare lay at the bottom of the hill where a stand impeded his progress and the hawker sitting at the counter curtained by hanging strips of pork gave a come-and-shop wave.

"Be heavier with the salt next time," Caderyn barked, slipping past the cart into an avenue.

Several blocks on, the avenue split into two streets islanding an apartment building. At the entrance sat a destitute old man. As Caderyn passed, the old man held out a weathered palm. Caderyn shook his head and entered the dust-caked lobby cluttered by busted clay dishes, worn-out clothing, and various unidentifiable debris. Wetness and decay had seeped into the stairs he took in timid steps. The landing creaked, too, and when he traversed the narrow hall, he feared the echoes of his boots announced the wealthy had come into the den of the desperate. This was not the slums, granted, but neither was Cilo's building situated among the mansiones in the affluent part of Polus.

Caderyn stopped at the fifth apartment. From within there was scraping and a woman shouting as if she was on her last nerve. He counted the doors to make sure he chose the right place as the woman grew angrier, her shrill orders coinciding with louder scraping. Then came what approximated as someone spanking a naked bottom, a child bawling. He raised a hand intending to knock then chose instead to scratch his forehead.

Wrong casa. Had to be. Even if Cilo got married in the months since they last saw each other, the cleptus would hardly abide a ready-made family, not with his profession.

"Cilo?" Caderyn yelled. And again. Once more.

The door swung open. A feral-looking brunette glared out, her bony body sporting a loincloth and a breast-strap. The cesta— a poorer, untailored version of a strophium—flattened her tits to the shapes of empty waterskins and cut into her sides.

He mumbled, "Cilo?"

"Not here. You go." She slammed the door in his face.

Miserable cunnus. Caderyn knocked, waited, knocked harder.

The woman flung open the door. Rosiness replaced the sallowness of her cheeks, blue eyes shining bright as an ocean on a sunny day.

"Cilo," insisted Caderyn.

"*Not* here. *You* go."

"Where is he?"

She gritted and bared brown teeth. "*Not—*"

"Here and I should go, aio. First tell me my friend's whereabouts."

"Friend dead. Clepta corpse."

Her assertion was a blow in the gut. "Dead...? When? How?"

"What when-how matter?" She tapped the side of her head. "You thick." Then sniffed. "*Phew.*"

The door's slamming boomed throughout the hallway. He lashed out with his foot, kicking the entrance open. There was a thud. A shriek. Before the woman could gather herself and come out from behind the door that had knocked her down, he barged into a room wherein a young girl rested upon a urine-stained mattress. Gouges marred the floor in front of her, the spike she had used clutched within her tiny fist. Snot ran over her lip. He scanned the wall and saw the hole for the spike from which the thief had hung his tools. The lone painting of harenarae fighting was absent as well. Like the tools and art that were gone so were the articles of clothing the thief folded and stacked under the window overlooking the avenue Caderyn had traveled.

The woman crept from behind the door wiping blood from her nose. "You no belong here. Friend dead."

A mouth that had gone dry turned his words into thick utterances. "For how long?"

"Last full moon." She pushed at his chest. "Daughter me live here now."

He retreated to the hall on heavy legs. "What happened?"

"Caught stealing. Died in—how you say square arena?— quadratum. But where make no difference. Neither when-how. Corpse never rebirth. You" —she waved as if shooing a fly— "go."

The door closed.

He stood and stared at nothing, willing himself to think of the same. After his mind blanked, he nodded, trod to and clumsily descended the stairs. Maybe he pushed too hard on the exit. Perhaps he walked faster than usual and huffed while departing this dilapidated, depressing neighborhood and it could have been just as true the embers of his temper burned hotter, the fire sparked by his entertaining thoughts of Lepidus. Maybe he wanted to rip apart the amphitheatrum the not-so-good folks of Bordia were building, what the world had heretofore never seen. Perhaps, too, he wanted to shove each block of stone straight up the snooty proconsul's natis. If there were sufficient strength within him, he would destroy every single damnable arena blotting the landscape of Calasade, squared and oval alike, although not so fast the monstrous fanatics of the festivities missed the opportunity to feel his blade.

Cocksuckers all.

He was still fuming mid-morning upon reaching the house Jacob—a fellow veteran and confidant— shared with a rich general under whom he and Caderyn had served in the Fors-Permia conflict. The general and Caderyn had once been good friends, too, but that friendship had eroded the farther Caderyn plummeted the social ladder. Nowadays the general snubbed him. Because this was not a man Caderyn could expect to extend hospitality, he timed his visits here according to the absence of Ducis Alexander. Today, however—at this hour—Alexander lorded over his clients within the tablinum. That central room featured excellent vantage points to the rest of the house and served as the passageway to the peristylium. It was there Jacob fulfilled his passion for horticulture tending to fuchsia, chrysanthemums, and lilies.

Caderyn lingered at the main entrance, listening to water gurgle out the mouth of a granite deity fountain embedded in the home's exterior painted burgundy on the bottom half and light brown at the top. Nothing else to be done for it. He swallowed the lump constituting his pride and hurried across the palatial grounds to the rear of the house and the servant's entrance. A gentle push opened the posticum with nary a squeak to reveal a corridor he slunk in a dozen quiet paces.

Peeking out into the peristylium, he spotted a brawny fellow out-of-place amidst such pretty scenery. The near-giant knelt on one knee. Water flowed from the spout of the pitcher he held and wetted a flowery bush.

"*Psst,*" hissed Caderyn.

Jacob's crown shone bright as he peered up. His goggling spanned the colonnade, bypassing the corridor.

"*Psst!*"

The glut put a finger in his ear and wiggled it.

"*Jacob.*"

"Huh?"

Caderyn stuck out his hand and retreated halfway along the corridor that darkened upon the big man entering. "Gather your gear. We have a job to do afar."

The ex-soldier hummed, rocked on the balls of his feet. "Cilo is dead."

"Aio." Caderyn let out a wavering sigh. "Do you know anyone who can serve as a replacement?"

"Mayhap. Meet me at Pulchra Virginem later this afternoon."

Caderyn swore under his breath.

"You detest the slums, this I know, but the colluvio is the only place we can find the person we need on such short notice. The one who can mayhap help us operates a roving group of lupae."

"Trust a leader of whores?" Caderyn rolled his eyes. "Only you. How well do you know this moderatrix?"

"Bathe." The big man sniffed, grinned. "For the sake of my blistering eyne, *bathe.*"

Caderyn smirked. "Anything else?"

"Stay sober. The stress in your face yells of drink. Now go. If Alexander sees you, he will raze his own domicile to erase the wake of your presence."

VII

QUAERO·

The Pulchra Virginem was a two-story ramshackle worse-for-wear in the five years Caderyn last visited the brothel. Then the conical thatch was new; now spaces exposed rafters and gaps separated once straight plank-walls. Windowpanes sitting in disjointed frames behind rusted bars cast milky reflections. If someone tried to peek within—as he was doing—that someone saw gauziness, which he did.

Snorting in disgusted wonder at Jacob's fascination with the seedy, Caderyn roved along the building-front and went through the entrance missing a door. When the "establishment" closed for the winter, the owner nailed a thick section of wood in place to protect what no one no matter how impoverished aspired to steal. Inside the Virginem were chest-high tables leaning on warped legs. A sign on the front of a slanting oak bar forbade in barely legible handwriting the smoking of tobacco or any other substance lest a spark set the Virginem aflame. Atop the bar were vegetables and fish of worrisome hues, the foodstuff piled in clay saucers, their edges chipped.

The pincernus grabbed what might have been a pepper slice in the distant past and plopped the black-green sliver between an orange mustache and beard, the beard wetting as he masticated and gave Caderyn glimpses of jagged, brown teeth. "What you want?"

Stay sober. He ordered water.

The pincernus sniffed. "Smell nice and had a bath, so why you want more aqua?"

"To keep my wits."

"You have wits and you came here?" The pincernus chuckled. "Takes every sort it does. Water here is used for dishes and washing cunnae between customers."

Alcohol being the lone available drink ranked as a top excuse among many Caderyn had used during the off-and-on sobriety. His and Elianna fighting, him getting stripped of honor and fired from investigating crimes. Somebody slighted him. Temperatures plummeted or soared. Today, should he order beer, Cilo's death served better than any. "Then give me naught. I will just wait."

"What for, sign from the gods?"

"My friend."

"You think this is a way-station? Order or scuttle."

In the seconds of silence that followed with the pincernus and Caderyn staring at each other, pressure built in Caderyn's temples. The hammer tapping on the inside of his forehead progressed to thumping. He fumbled the copper coin dug from his pouch. "Cervisia. Clean mug."

The pincernus scooped up the aes. He went into the storage chamber behind the bar and returned carrying two bowl-sized cups filled to their brims. The rich appearance of the honey-tinted beer was surprising.

Typical, Caderyn thought, the single thing of quality in this shit-tavern is the alcohol. "I ordered one."

"Unus aes, duo cervisae."

As if the cup were a newborn babe, Caderyn lifted the beer to his nose and lingered in an anticipatory moment very similar to those electrifying ones in which he had waited to kiss Elianna, their mouths close enough for her breath to warm his lips. When had they last done that? Years ago, the day he saw her off to a new job. Late in the eve she arrived home from working as a fullo and stinking of ammonia to trip over him half-unconscious and sprawled out in their hovel. She had gasped his name, holding up hands blistered and pruned after washing garments, her face red and sweat-stained, golden hair tied in knots, her heartbreak evident in her crumpled, quivering chin and the glisten of utter pity in her darkening and moistening green eyes.

He swore then again *never again.*

As he did now clutching the cup's twin and retreating to a table beneath the milky window of a distant wall. The beers Caderyn placed in the table's center, trying his best to ignore the barley-scent by playing witness to meager activity that grew more interesting towards dusk when a quintet of rough-looking men kept glancing at him. Their conversational tone of boisterous became conspiratorial.

"Upon his leave..."

"Aio. Then we......You grab his pouch."

"Outside...get him...take swords."

The shadow of a large head and broad shoulders fell across the tabletop Caderyn leaned against.

Jacob offered a tense smile. "Are they discussing you?"

"Unfortunate they are drunk. A good fight is a welcome distraction from—" Sighing, Caderyn jabbed at the beers.

"Do as in the old days and start the melee yourself."

"Mayhap I have matured."

"Here I thought we would go gray afore that happened."

"Whereas I shall be silver-haired, you will have lost the horseshoe that half-circles your noggin."

Jacob guzzled the cups and emitted a loud belch. "Is your worry eased?"

"Much. How long must we wait in this sewer?"

"Until after the moderatrix puts on a show. It is she I believe can point us towards a thief."

"Entertainment?" Caderyn wrinkled his nose. "In this cobweb-infested hole?"

"Do not turn your eyne from the finer side of life."

"Finer? You lose the ability to discern."

Jacob slapped him on the shoulder. "Have I not explained myself?"

"Nulla."

"But during our skirmishes against Permia, the jobs we did, I—?"

"You, Jacob, are tight-lipped regarding your past. The only subject."

The big man arched his eyebrows. "Blabber, do I?"

"Like an old woman with little else to bide her time."

"Is there naught you speculate?"

Caderyn shrugged. "You wish for neither wife nor children or even a place of your own. Hence, why you stay with Ducis Alexander. A capable fighter if somewhat slow due to your size, you are the sole man I trust with my life now that Cilo has died."

"And?"

"You are a first or second generation citizen."

"What makes you say this?"

He exhaled hard to rid his nostrils of the alcohol on Jacob's breath. "Your given name is of foreign origin."

"So is yours."

"Aio," he confirmed, a little embarrassed. "My parens named me after a man who saved my uncle's life. A servus. Were your mother and father peregrinae?"

"They were. They came to these lands destitute and settled here in the colluvio."

"You say 'colluvio' as if these neighborhoods are special."

Jacob bobbed his head. "My pater once said, 'Son, upon a man leaving where he grew up, he is free to purchase a new house, but can never choose a new home.' Verum, I love the colluvio."

"By the gods, what is wrong with you?"

"Naught." The big man sniggered. "Think of it this way. Although colluvionis people are poorer than my general and *most* of my friends, they are also forthright. Them living here are too consumed by the prospect of eating for pretending to be something other than what they are." He gestured to the men who had been discussing robbing Caderyn. "Them, right off, you can tell they are your enemy. They will not convince you to befriend them so they might steal everything you value, including your self-worth. All they want is your coin. They may take your life should you fight, but such is the way and that is as it should be."

"A harsh view."

"Comes from living in a harsh world."

Caderyn licked his lips, denied himself wiping them. "Why not just say you were raised here?"

"Well" —the big man blushed— "mayhap I do carry on."

"Appreciation for your faith. By your armor and sword, the bedroll slung across your back, I see you are joining me, yet have not asked of the task afar or the coin it pays."

"I differ from those short on height and patience and do not badger."

"Badger, do I?"

"Like a suspicious wife."

Caderyn snickered. "A couple of women are we then. Come the morrow's morn we ride to Dahak and from there sail to Bordia. We are to learn what happened to a proconsul's...I am unsure what she is to him."

Jacob furrowed his brow. "Why do you need me and a cleptum?"

"We may have to take her back through force, mayhap stealth. Ten thousand chrysae."

"I *hate* horses, but you put up a lot of gold. Count me in."

"I already—"

A woman entered the Virginem, her arms raised overhead and wrists crossed, hips swaying. Her blue wig swung to the small of her back over a pale yellow strophium cut low in the center that was as see-through as the skirt belted around her waist. The tunica intima covered little of her thighs and revealed her black pubis hairs, the curves of her hips and ass when she spun to the beat a youthful toga-wearer trailing her banged out on a handheld drum. Three women undernourished and dressed identical to Blue Wig emerged from the darkness. The trio encircled their leader, grabbing each other's hands, the shawls they held creating a curtain that veiled Blue Wig undressing. The crowd cheered her writhing silhouette. First she threw her strophium and second, her tunica intima. The curtain parted. Nude, the moderatrix traded places with another dancer.

Same routine of undressing and tossing clothes.

Same men contesting for the discarded articles.

The woman within the shawls stood for another and she another; the fourth. Drummer Boy slowed his tempo as the naked quartet fanned out holding hands.

Blue Wig on the end jiggled her tits before raising the hand of the attractive young woman standing beside her. "Who pays for Polyxena?"

"Five coppers," someone shouted.

Another bellowed, "Ten."

"Twenty."

The room quieted except for Drummer Boy patting out a lethargic cadence.

Blue Wig scoffed. "Twenty aera is a pittance. This beauty has such a mouth it will drain your cock for days. I insist upon thirty."

"Aio," Five Coppers hollered. "Thirty."

"She is yours." Blue Wig pulled at Polyxena to get her moving.

Caderyn frowned and said to Jacob, "Are there no rooms nearby?"

"Nulla. This is the show I mentioned. Part of that is us watching sex take place between the lupae and winning bidder. Gets the crowd in a fervor and amounts to greater coin. Saturnina, she of the blue horsehair, is no stranger to selling cunnae."

"Are all her lupae women? That one—the one whose arm she strokes—looks to be a girl."

Blue Wig—Saturnina—smiled and moved behind the waifish teenager. The madam rested her chin on the girl's bony shoulder and cupped the girl's pear-sized breasts. "Such delicate fruit, men, silky skin. Who pays fifty aera to fututio Isaura?"

The crowd hushed.

Saturnina coyly smiled. "This apple is fresh from the tree, aio, no doubt. Unbitten? Uh-huh. Who pays fifty?" A painted nail targeted Caderyn. "You, beast?"

He shook his head.

Her nail bypassed Jacob and pointed at a bearded man standing at the next table. "You who spies out the corner of his eyne, tell me the last time you partook of such wondrous purity."

Side Glancer mumbled.

"What is that? Let us hope your cock is not as soft as your voice." Saturnina shut her mouth until the crowd stopped guffawing. "*Speak.*"

The man cleared his throat.

"Never?" Now it was Saturnina laughing. "Poor cock of yours—"

"Sixty," a different man cried, coming forward from the bar.

"Mmm, mayhap a fair offer, but let us make sure. This labia..." Saturnina stroked between the girl's legs. She brought the finger to her nose and sniffed, then licked the tip. "*Untainted. Wet.* Did you say sixty aera? Silly brute. That amount is an insult."

"Jacob," muttered Caderyn. "This is—"

"The colluvio where life is *real.*"

Saturnina pinched Isaura's nipple. "How much silver, silly brute, to suck this mamilla?"

"Fifteen bigatae," answered the man from the bar.

She redirected her attention to Side Glancer. "What say you? Will you go sixteen? For cunnus so tight it might squish your cock, assuming said cock is not a stick."

"Prove that claim," someone shouted.

Saturnina put a palm over the girl's pubic mound and moved her middle finger back until the finger vanished and the girl squirmed.

"Aio, sixteen." Side Glancer grabbed the girl around the waist and hauled her through a parting of the crowd, its applause almost overriding the girl's sobbing.

Caderyn groped for his mucrones.

"Stop," Jacob ordered. "You would kill a handful, but die in the end for a lupa who volunteered, as Saturnina's women do. This is how they provide for themselves and their families."

He stowed his weapons, gulped to repudiate the sourness coating his tongue. Bile.

"Last, gentleman" —Saturnina motioned to the final whore— "we have a rare treat. Hear me as I declare your sword shall not penetrate Quirina's theca. That sheath she reserves for her husband. Neither will your cock slip betwixt these lovely lips." Saturnina kissed the woman. "Show them, honey, the sweet natis they bid upon."

Quirina twirled and bent, parting her cheeks and displaying her anus.

Saturnina cackled, thrusting her hips back-and-forth. "Paedico!"

The applause thundered at such volume Caderyn was at a loss how Saturnina judged the greatest bid. Nor did he see the winner. By then he glared at the floor, wincing every time he heard the virgin shriek for her patron to quit hurting her.

"Jacob," he choked. "Find me outside."

Upon exiting Caderyn shoved anyone in his path. Fresh air helped him breathe but did nothing for clearing his head. He drifted farther and farther from the entryway. When the urge to rush back in and save the girl had lessened to a drone, he stopped and stared at the night-sky. He wondered if it were true, that the twinkling up there were the gods' eyes blinking, and if so, why those deities favored watching cruelty. Did seeing the innocent get mistreated by the perverse amuse them? Why was it strife rather than peace which proved entertaining?

Jacob exited late reporting there was a short walk ahead of them. Saturnina had recommended a talented thief staying at an hospitium in Emporium Antica, the market-road where once stood the city's finest shops during Polus's first few centuries.

Caderyn got going, uncaring whether Jacob followed. Upon reaching at the corner of Antica, he judged the rampart lining the avenue was the only commonality the modern-day alleyway held with the antiquated. Merchant stores, smiths, tanners, and odorous stables yet existed though were a pale shadow of their forebears. A majority of the road had holes and made making nighttime navigation a challenging, knee-jarring affair. Several buildings down, he went under a lopsided sign featuring a weathered painting of a bed. The lobby smelled of mildew. An old man—presumably the innkeeper—slept on one of four grimy red sofas.

Jacob came to Caderyn's side and pointed at the staircase. "Second floor, fourth room."

"The cleptus goes by Mathis?"

"Aio."

At the middle landing Caderyn turned and stomped up the remaining steps, ascending to and marching along a hallway overlooking the lobby. He halted, lifted a fist, and pounded. Dirt cascaded from the ceiling.

Someone within grumbled.

He kept knocking.

Faint steps developed into clomps that preceded the door swinging open. Caderyn saw no one in front of him, instead eyed the cracked wall on the other side of the room.

"Hah," Jacob blurted. "Saturnina led us astray. Here I request a cleptus and she refers us to a Trux just tall enough to root my navel. Look at the beads on him, how he sweats even at night. Is what happens to diminutive bastards from the farthest northern mountains."

Caderyn looked down at the thief with ash-colored hair who glared upward from between puffy eyelids. Gray eyes moving at a snail's pace took Jacob and him in from toes-to-head.

"An ogre," said the cleptus, "and a muscle-bound swine. Makes no difference we share a friend. Valet."

Caderyn stuck out a palm to keep Mathis from shutting the door.

The short, handsome man with a wide forehead tugged on the waistband of his half-breeches and scratched his somewhat hairy chest. "You, swine, carry mucrones. Harenarius or ex-soldier?"

Jacob grunted. "Do not answer him. He is a meddlesome cur too tiny for our needs. I say any of his trade staying in this lousy hospitium is unable to pry a babe from its mater's tit."

Mathis tipped his chin at Caderyn. "What do you want?"

"Help in rescuing a woman kidnapped. Come the dawn we travel to Dahak and board a ship going to Floridus. Regio Bordia."

"Permia is my homeland."

"Mayhap you know a man named Lepidus."

"Nulla."

Ah well, Caderyn thought, his glimmer of hope for learning more about the proconsul withering. "He is the nobilis who hired me. One thousand chrysae is yours for your company."

"And if my services are necessary?"

"Your pay tripled." He tilted his thumb outward. "This is Jacob." Then at himself. "I am Caderyn."

"Upon sunrise. Brute, *ogre*." Proffering a taunting grin, Mathis shut the door.

"Prickly shrub," Jacob remarked. "Could be a mistake conscripting him."

Caderyn shouldered past the big man. "I imagine there are cleptae in Floridus."

"So why not wait to hire one there?"

"Because here gives me the chance to know the thief without first putting a girl's life in his hands." He peeked over the bannister to find the innkeeper still slept. "Seek out undisturbed dust in front of a door and stay in that room."

"The hour is early. Let us find vinum for me and aqua for you."

"Go to bed, Jacob, and leave me alone."

"You sound upset. The Virginem?"

"A stupid question." Caderyn balled his hands into fists. "I always knew your tastes bordered on the distasteful, but...ah, Jacob, you shame me."

VIII

PRAEDO⊙

Dust sullied the floor of the room Caderyn chose, its nightstand, the storage chest where he placed his swords and clothing while undressing. As with the lobby, there was mildew; strongest in the concaved bed he laid upon. He let go of his money pouch but kept it within easy reach at his hip and closed his eyes, sighed, tried to fall asleep.

Ticks of the inn settling differed from those of his hovel. No breeze whistled through gaps in the planks. Neither did crickets chirp. Strange what a man missed, the very things which irritated him. What had Jacob said? A home deserted was gone for eternity. Such as the villa he had purchased for Elianna. Trips back in time to capture lost chances and fulfill empty promises, to save those due to die were impossibilities. He considered the virginal lupa and remembered her cries of anguish, how he had done nothing except get away, just as two years into the Fors-Permia conflict after overhearing members of his battalion ravaging the boy.

When he reported what happened to Ducis Alexander, the general berated him. "What is it you wish me to do? These are the spoils of war."

The injustice of the perpetrators evading punishment had been the start of Caderyn's descent. Dismal years, a ruined marriage, and the ultimate tragedy had passed before he understood the sole person from whom he needed clemency was the man in his reflection. The soldiers raping the boy numbered too many for him to fight. The virginal lupa could not be protected from her own choices. Here, under the guise of darkness, his soul bared and memories unobstructed, he admitted coin was the secondary reason for agreeing to rescue Indrasena. Within her salvation rested his own. Maybe afterwards he would imagine his wife happy rather than recall her torment born of his failures as a husband.

He breathed deep, commanded the muscles in his body to relax, drifted...

...Into blackness, serenity, floated in nothing, unmoving. Legions marched. Men fought. Swords glittered under the sun. Bodies lay dismembered on blood-soaked battlefields. Sky, trees, a villa. Through the compluvium he went into the atrium, coasted to a peristylium with a lush garden. Elianna's intoxicating laughter passed through him leaving behind a chill. Horses in stables neighed. Blackness, serenity. Inertness. Clouds pluming. Forests and fields, mountains, lakes, rivers. An ocean. Island.

Boards creaking?

Someone had entered his room. He was sure of that before spotting the cloaked figure darting into the hall. Caderyn groped for the pouch. Gone. He rolled off the bed and grabbed a mucro. Out the room he dashed after the thief.

Was it Mathis who already descended the stairs?

Too speedy to know, too speedy to catch following in the cleptus's path. Caderyn vaulted over the bannister, letting his knees absorb the impact of the floor rushing to meet him, and tucked his head against his shoulder, pressing the mucro broadside against his torso as he rolled into a sofa. No sooner had he stopped than he gained his feet and ran.

The cleptus sprinting for the exit looked back—not Mathis— bumped into the door, and faltered. Caderyn was on him, grappling the cleptus's cloak, yanking with all his might, sending the man airborne. The nimble bastard landed then pirouetted and pulled a pair of short-swords from scabbards at his hips. The weapons would have carved Caderyn had he not bobbed side-to-side. On his third dodge he doubled over. The thief kicked him in the chin and shot off stars in his vision. Unable to see more than blurs through the watering of his eyes, he could still hear the whooshing blade coming for him, but leaned away too slow.

The sword gashed his upper arm.

He raised his mucro, blocking further incursions while pummeling the thief's gut. When he got the smaller man to retreat, Caderyn bounded and swung downward, the iron bulb of his mucro's hilt clouting the thief on top of the head. He smashed a roundhouse punch into the thief's jaw. A third. Fourth. The cleptus lunged, stabbing with both swords.

Twisting so the blades passed on either side of him, Caderyn released his blade and grappled the thief's wrists. His head-butting the man dazed and forced him to drop his weapons. Whoever the thief, he was tough, grunting in a dissatisfying way every time he was struck as Caderyn slugged him right-left, left-right.

Mayhap, he thought, I will need kill him—something he wished to avoid so as to discover how the thief knew of his presence and coin pouch.

His loss of concentration cost him and gave the faster man an opportunity to retaliate. The thief's volley of short jabs hurt far less than the boot he drove into Caderyn's groin that dropped him into a fetal position. Cold sweats came. Cramps were crippling, bouts of pain nauseating. He shut his eyes and rocked, listened to the thief's running diminish and an old man hollering, who must have been Jacob thundering down the steps.

IX

AПIMUS

In that semiconscious void dividing wakefulness and sleep she fought. The pit's hardened floor was a good armament for keeping sleep at bay, but the best weapons she had at her disposal were battleaxes in the form of herbs cooking outside the pit, those scents terrific for warding off the nightmares that accompanied rest. Daggers included shrills of laughing gulls and the tide and trees rustling, the growling and grunting of beasts, gray-skins chattering incomprehensible foreign words, and fires crackling. She groaned from the effort of sitting up, then from the stench emanating out her armpits and the heady putridity wafting from between her legs.

Piss maybe or an infection.

At least she had eaten nothing to spur the emptying of her bowels. For that she thanked the gods, though at the same time— oh, how she wished for the smallest morsel to reduce the chasm in her gut.

And water. She could use a bucket of water. Tens of buckets. Tens and tens and little hens clucking around the bend. Tens and tens of little hens—

The banging of drums cut short her titter, yanked her away from falling off the edge of sanity and into momentary lunacy. Gray-skin verses similar to chants of uneducated servae attempting witchcraft added a layer to the cacophony. She stared upward, waiting. For what she was unsure but somehow knew something *important* would happen.

And it did.

Smoke rose beyond the edge of the pit's mouth. Not the regular billowing smoke that bloomed at the top, no; this column appeared shorn on the sides—as if a column of glass encased it—and presented a rainbow of changing colors that stopped in a flash of white. The white darkened to ash which deepened to a charcoal tint as the drumbeats and chanting settled into a cyclical, unremitting clatter that sped up and intensified into dizzying repetitions.

The pit imprisoning her expanded. Shrunk. Its walls thinned. *Vanished.* Before her stretched blue firmament. Beneath the sky lay fields and mountains.

How could that be?

She shut her eyes.

And still saw.

Saw herself standing atop a huge boulder within a valley, throngs of beasts rushing past on either side. With a smile born of madness she raised a staff overhead and commanded the beasts to go to war in a guttural dialect she *knew* but did not know.

That snippet was all the nightmare she wanted—must have fallen asleep and this was a terrible dream. She rent open her eyes. The column of smoke that had risen high above the tallest trees ceased going upward and curved near the top, becoming hook-shaped. The tip directed towards her, slithering on its way to filling the pit and carpeting the floor, hiding her lower body and torso prior to swirling about her head. She searched for ~~something~~ *anything* to block off her nose and mouth, protect her burning throat. The coughing fit that hit and sent her staggering sapped what little strength she still had. She reached for an outcropping of rock to use as support and missed, fell; was falling, falling,

falling. Landed face-first. Whiteness again flared, this time in her mind's eye amid the blast of pain coming from her forehead. It was bleeding. She stared numbly at her red-painted fingertips that blurred as they drifted away and melded into the charcoal mist.

Unconsciousness overtook her.

More visions of the beasts—her father had called them bimembrae—that glared with their ferocious eyes and glowing orange irises. Protruding jowls. Their fangs nipped, bit, devoured. She screamed herself awake and was horrified to find her prison smokeless.

Was she imagining things? Had she gone off the edge after all?

No.

It...whatever *it* was...was still happening. Gray-skins were yelling. Their choppy words escaped her understanding but the underlying fear did not. She struggled to stand, scampered to the pit's side. There she flinched at the recurrent clanking of metal on metal and cringed from howls not quite wolf, almost human that started in a low pitch and decorated her skin in goose-bumps. Gray-skin bellows took on elements of higher alarm.

She put her palms over her face.

And spied spearheads clanging against bars, getting jabbed into the cage. Those damnable weapons stabbed the animal. Another howl. Drawn out, weaker. She bit hard on her chapped bottom lip and pawed her thighs. The beast roared. A cage rattled. The imprisoned bimembrus grappling the cage's bars using paw-like hands possessing three fingers and a thumb rocked the cage. Panic mounted in gray-skin shouts as some of them strained to keep the cage on the ground while others of their kind kept stabbing their spears. In hearing the beast's deathly howl, she doubled over, wrapped her arms that were little thicker than the bones within them around herself. Spears and more spears stuck the beast. Blood ran as streams. A haunted roar ending in a slow fadeout dropped her to her knees.

The bimembrus was dead.

Miserable, low, merciless monsters the gray-skins, how they cheered before quieting.

When footsteps approached her prison, she flattened against the pit's far wall, thinking if whoever came planned to throw spears or shoot arrows at her, she would move again as her assailant maneuvered, forcing him to jump in after her so she might rake his face for what they had done.

A triangular blob sailed overhead and thudded to the pit's floor, splattering muddy red drops. Inexplicably drawn, she crept forward mindless to the danger of venturing into the open.

What had been tossed in was the size of a baby and bulged in its yellowish middle, oozed thick crimson out a dark purple bottom and leaked rivulets from small tubes. Along the wider, sallow top sprouted a pair of broader nozzles conjoining into a conduit matching her wrist's circumference. The knife used to cut out the organ must have been sharp. Arteries were thick and spongy. Their even-severed ends smelled of iron.

"Int-rah-seen-ah." The gray-skin mispronouncing her name stood at the pit's mouth and was adorned in leather breeches. Bracers protecting his forearms, horned pauldrons his shoulders, and a breastplate were of the same material. A wild patch of black hair carpeted his head. At this range, with the advantages of light and a prolonged look, she could tell his forehead slanted back at a sharp angle from the pronounced ridge of his brow. Violet-colored tattoos on his cheeks formed elaborate swirl patterns. He gestured at the animal part. "Eeeet."

Her brother had done so with the heart of a lion. After the ritual failed to spark her brother's ability to control the cats, Pater requested Indrasena undergo the ordeal. She wished she could tell the gray-skins what she had her father.

I will sooner starve.

— X —

ABITUS

Blood from Caderyn's wound streamed down his arm and over the back of his hand, between his knuckles and fingers to drop and splatter while he waited for Jacob to fetch a bandage from the inn's supply room. A disastrous day and night, what with learning of Cilo's death, witnessing the doleful lupa, recalling the boy, getting beaten in a fight against a smaller opponent. He had never needed a drink this bad. Now, because a thief had stolen his money, he was unable to afford a single cervisia at Pulchra Virginem. How to cover the costs of a bedroll, food? Beg Jana for an advance? He spat pink saliva and wiped his mouth several times with his unbloodied palm.

Aio, a horrible day and night.

Jacob exited the supply room behind the staircase, strips of bandages in hand. "Are you worried over coin?"

Caderyn smirked.

"Mayhap," the big man said grinning, "some will pay to fututio your virgin natis. I doubt you will raise as much as the girl, but still."

Another wipe; this one stung. "Do you take so light the virtuous ravaged?"

"Virtuous? You being your age and this unwitting..." Jacob shook his head. "The girl was pure in body, aio, but not in soul. How else do you explain the girl's selling herself to the highest bidder?"

"And what of the boy, Jacob?"

"Ah, there *it* is. War is madness. Let go the memory."

"Would that I could."

"You could if you ceased tormenting yourself." Jacob patted him on the cheek, like a parent humoring their child. "Life is unforgiving and ugly. Take that to heart and struggle less."

"Your soul is iron."

"None should be otherwise. Quit this self-pitying and let me tend to the wound I can fix." The strips of bandages Jacob applied were tight and measured, similar to how he talked. "Your problem is you view everyone as a victim, yourself included. Grow up. In this world there are just the weak and the strong. To save one from the other does not fall upon you." He tied off the bandage, went about cleaning his own hands with a rag using short, angry motions. "The boy getting taken has caused you greater pain than it ever did him and yours has lasted longer. Those soldiers were too many. There was naught to do. What gets me is your *knowing* these things and yet, you berate yourself."

"Finished?"

"With what your pride will allow."

Caderyn retrieved his mucro, stomped to and up the stairs. Of the people aware he was at this inn only Mathis could find someone to rob him on such short notice. He did not bother knocking but kicked open the door, so sure of the thief's absence and that absence pointing to culpability he at first neglected to see the diminutive man jerking from his slumber and scrambling for a short-sword atop the nightstand.

"Touch it," Caderyn shouted, "and you lose that hand. Where is my coin?"

"Something goes missing and I am to blame? Right unfair if you ask me."

"I did not. Few had knowledge of my presence here and fewer still of my carrying coin." He closed to within swinging distance and slung a hard right to the thief's chin, felling Mathis back onto the bed. Caderyn pounced, grappling a fistful of the thief's hair and putting the edge of a mucro to the man's throat. "A single chance. I give you that to tell me who took my pouch." He pressed the sword. Its edge piercing the thief's skin just beneath the lump in his throat made talking difficult, but that was okay; the nick got the message across.

Mathis's upper lip furled on one side. Sweat beaded his forehead as his cheeks paled. "Whatever coin...gone," he croaked, "is less valuable than...paid trip home. Who...led you...here? Think!"

Saturnina.

Jacob—as per his nature—had spouted off to the moderatrix why they required a plagiarius and the pay was substantial. Caderyn should have asked about the conversation given its lengthiness, but was too incensed by the lupi show to ask. Neither had he troubled himself regarding the source of intermittent noise behind them during their walk to the inn. A tap here, a scuffle there, he realized, had been someone trailing them to learn in what rooms they stayed so Saturnina's cleptus knew which to pilfer.

Crestfallen, he got off Mathis and shuffled out onto the balcony. Jacob hollered up, asking what had happened. Ignoring the query and continuing to inside his own room, Caderyn wiped his arm and dressed before perching on the bed, sitting with his back to the window. He put a hand on each knee, squeezed hard enough to hurt.

The morning warmth coming through the window stated he was tardy for meeting Jana. The hour was thus too late to locate Saturnina and recover what he lost, too late for avoiding shame or saving his marriage and Elianna, too late for everything except giving up and selling his gear and descending the spiral staircase. To have beer bubble in his mouth; wonderful—the fizziness always relaxed him, made him feel as if he floated upon a lazy stream, he uncaring of the stream's destination. What did that matter when the journey was pleasant?

Blissful oblivion. How he missed—

Every god as his witness, he was *sick* of this constant needling that bled his soul a prick at a time. His yearning was stronger today than yesterday, this month than last, this year than those prior. To battle his desire was a painful go-around without end or point. Why fight when he questioned for whom he fought and the reason to continue? Drunks got alleviated of spiritual tearing, were oblivious to the grief they planted in those they loved and the harm they brought onto themselves. Sobriety let a person fret, buried him shovelful after vindictive shovelful in steaming piles of mementos, constant reminders he had not lived up to expectations, including his own.

He should have hidden the coin. Idiotic and naïve thinking the money-pouch secure at his hip. Retarded blaming Mathis when he should have known who was behind the theft the second he discovered his pouch gone and...

...The blade of his mucro with its metallic sheen was never more inviting. How often had he put the tip of his sword in that soft bit of flesh at the base of his neck, where a quick and powerful stab would end his suffering? How many times? Five, ten, twenty? Why had he always been incapable of completing the act? Cowardice? Shame? No basis for either. Elianna ignorant of his actions would be unhurt by them. Separated now, separated always. There was the Afterlife and the Afterdeath, a promise-land reserved for the honorable and an abyss consuming the fallen, the broken.

What was he other than depraved and shattered?

Weak.

A man who had taken off on an adventure and returned with a trunkful of gold, acting a hero. He had not gone home straightaway to his wife. Oh, no. He went to the Twisted Vine. Had to celebrate, get satiated on drink and the thrill of playing Imperatori against a professional gambler. Come dawn Caderyn had lost his last coin. He begged for a loan and a chance to win his money back through dice-poker. The gambler complied, lent him three thousand chrysae, but Caderyn's luck at Numeri was poorer than it had been with strategy, the loan disappearing faster than it took a strong breeze to blow the white fluff off a dandelion. The gambler conceded a fortnight for Caderyn to settle the debt plus an additional five hundred gold in interest.

Caderyn went without work in the three weeks that passed and failed on his promise of restitution. The gambler, though, made good on his oath of ramification.

Nighttime. Moon shining bright. A pool of crimson took on a blue-purple hue in such light. She sprawled on the dirt floor of their hovel, a knife embedded in her gut. The killer could have been merciful and sliced upward to finish her, but the gambler had intended for Elianna to survive just long enough for Caderyn to reach his wife and hear her final, soul-jarring declaration. He had expected hatred and blame to lace her proclamation. Turned out there were crueler things than what might cause him to despise himself tenfold.

Become the man I love.

Those were her words. Her awful, awful, haunting words. They were why he refused to forget the boy, why he would recall in the future the virginal lupa and her screams. His focusing on the atrocities he did not stop was less hurtful than fixating on his wife's murder and who was responsible. No, he had not been the man to stab her, though he may as well have been. His stupidity was the driving-force for the blade that had stuck her.

A knock—no break to grieve or rest, thank the gods. With a groan Caderyn got his sore body moving, sheathed his swords, and put on their harness. He opened the door, loathing the pitiful expression on the face looking downward at him.

"What of Mathis?" he said to Jacob, slipping past.

"Ready and no less annoying than when we met him." The big man's voice dropped to a hush. "I paid the cupo for our rooms. You need coin—"

"Nulla."

"—to get you by until Lepidus—"

"I will not go into debt. For *any* reason. To anyone."

"But—"

Caderyn squared his shoulders. Too ashamed to greet Mathis and apologize, he headed for the exit, noting the lighter footsteps that accompanied Jacob's. At least the thief was joining them. That was something.

Emporium Antica in the morning differed from the street he had blundered along in the dark. Still present was the hopelessness that the derelict buildings secreted. Holes in the road yet went unfilled, but new were the colluvionum shoppers bustling in front of merchants selling vegetables, fruits, and meats on wooden blocks that stood navel-high. Most offensive were the scents of unwashed clothes and bodies that prevailed even over manure as he passed the stables and confronted a merchant rearranging a pile of shiny and wet fish to hide those that had lost their silvery luster.

The fish-hawker took a pinch of salt from a bowl and spread it over his stock, the hanging skin of his jowls jiggling. Whiskers peppered his cheeks and chin. His sly grin was perfect for swaying undecided shoppers.

"Caught from the River Canalis this morn," claimed the merchant.

Caderyn hustled around the corner, wanting nothing from water contaminated by sewage and refuse, including the occasional floating corpse. Plebes scampered along the next street industrial with its smelting metal and hammering of steel and iron. The homes in poor repair depressed him as much as the old men and women huddling in doorways extending grubby, upturned palms. Late-morning he, Jacob, and Mathis marched on shaded walkways fronting domiciles well-constructed that underwent frequent maintenance. Avenues here were brighter and cleaner.

He stopped at a fork in the road, pondering which offshoot led to Via Arcadia and the marketplace where he planned to trade his gear for something of inferior quality and coin. He turned to Jacob. "Direct me to the Mercatus."

The big man sighed going left. Caderyn fell in beside Mathis and struggled for something to say. Three streets later he grumbled out an awkward apology.

Replied the diminutive man, shrugging, "I have faced worse treatment. In Elasai..."

They parted to go around a sectioned-off monument honoring the god of fertility. Bronze molded into the shape of a gargantuan snake coiled around a wrought column. The statue was a serpent in body whereas its head was that of a horse, its mane flowing to scales in thick, twisting locks.

Once the fence enclosing Serpentis ended, Caderyn rejoined Mathis. "Your race is uncommon south of the great mountains. How did Permia come to be your homeland?"

"My parents left the Trux nation of Metallum afore birthing me and never said why. Thus I am unsure. Mayhap they got ousted because of their religious beliefs, believing in unpopular gods. Such is common there from what I gather."

"You mentioned Elasai. True the capital city sits on an ocean's shore and is made of ivory?"

"Not ivory but stone polished white. You can see the city on a clear day miles out on Ocean Caeruli. Come to think of it, you can see Antheral miles ahead in blackness, too. Huge lanterns burn atop the city-wall to appease Ignis."

The fire-god; a fitting icon for the southernmost state that once ruled all Calasade. "A long way from Permia or here for that matter. What was your business there?"

"A member of Elasai's Lux Latum requested my services by means of a mutual friend. The member wanted information on an associate to blackmail her into backing a controversial tax law."

"Were you successful?"

"Nulla. I made the mistake of visiting a tabernum in the finer part of Antheral. Nobilia drunk and in the mood for entertainment insisted I dance for them. After I refused, their slaves beat me until I got right close to Death.

"Upon healing I decided to go back to the cooler weather and friendlier people of Permia. I got as far north here in Fors as Polus afore my money ran out. So here I did what small jobs came my way, spreading the word I wanted something bigger as long as that something bigger did not involve the city's guilds." Mathis clucked his tongue. "I was happy to take advantage of your proposition, even if" —he tipped his chin at Jacob and squinted— "one is a heartless ogre and you" —the thief grimaced, pointing at Caderyn— "you battle demons and suffer because of it. Your hands shake if they are idle. When they are not, they wipe your mouth."

"I am surprised you took my offer."

"Desperate times," Mathis said, his smile wide, "call for desperate people. My hope is we save the girl and get paid, but whatever happens, I will have received a free return to my homeland."

They trailed Jacob into a small alley and onto the Mercatus. Therein the square-mile pushcarts and wagons interspersed alongside and between stationary stalls. Canopies creating a medley of dizzying colors rippled in the breeze over customers of every social paradigm bustling here, bustling there, oohing and awing, selling, purchasing, always bartering. Caderyn's gaze swept the buildings enclosing the market and lingered on a banner draping a taberni storefront.

That was the place. Not now but *very* soon.

He made his way into the crowd and pushed-twisted-sidestepped to the center of the Mercatus. Two of the smiths — Arma de Gaius and Metalli de Polus— sold ware equal or superior to his. Beneath the canopy of the third smith, the Ferrum Merx, stood racks of iron swords.

Caderyn laid his mucrones on the Merx's counter. "These are steel," he informed the boney proprietor. "I will trade them for a pair iron-made and coin."

Skinny inspected Caderyn's weapons, tracing the blades, lifting them, turning them, the gleam in his eyes reminiscent of a vulture watching an animal dying. "How much?"

"One hundred chrysae." Perhaps his throat was too tight; the proprietor showed no sign of having heard. "I said one—"

"Fifty."

"Are you a smith or circumscriptus? My blades are pattern-forged. The demand is *firm*." Sweeping a forearm across his mouth, Caderyn longed to near the tabernum, succumb to its seduction. "Heed the following well. Try again to swindle me" — *wipe-wipe-wipe*— "I will bring you pain."

Skinny held up a palm. "A hundred it is."

The swords Caderyn got in the exchange could chip, break, or warp. Their blades weighed heavy and made prolonged battles or accurate striking harder than what his pattern-forged weapons did. Not that it mattered; no upcoming battles for him. Were Jacob absent, Caderyn would have outright sold his high-quality blades, but with his big friend present and acting the watchdog, he needed the ruse to cover his true intentions.

Skinny counted out the coins and put them in a pouch, handing over the things of consequence. The transaction finished, Caderyn nodded and went back the way he had come, walking in a normal pace until mingling with the crowd. Then he darted around people to the sound of Jacob shouting after him. Caderyn ran faster, broke from the throngs, and skidded to a halt at the taberni doorway.

Breathless, he huffed for air, taking in alcohol's unmistakable odor.

Did the tabernum offer Imperatori, house someone rich unaware their luck had transformed? Had his? An ache massive in its hollowing pushed him to play, to drink, and forget *her*, forget how Elianna's blood-smeared body had lain, her legs askew, the protruding knife, her gurgling whisper.

Become the man I love.

He had tried, tried his utmost to grant her wish and develop into the kind of person she admired; such had been his motivation for sobriety. Why continue this losing struggle with Elianna dead?

Oblivion awaited.

XI

INTERLUDIUM

Sevum de Nonus, a.CDXCIX

Left from Dahak at sunrise w/full cargo & 4 passengers. Jana Lepidus among passengers 4 return 2 Floridus. Traveled w/us on initial voyage per command of Abelardus Lepidus, proconsul of Regio Bordia. Bad luck 2 have woman aboard due 2 disruptions her sex causes on ship full of men, but have no choice. Good thing journey 2 Floridus is short & crew was satiated by lupae in Dahak.

Must B noted irate fellow accompanies her along w/2 other men. Do not fully comprehend trouble between them. Overheard enough 2 venture guess. Man called Caderyn Fortis wanted 2 quit job. Came unwillingly. 'Coerced' by rather large companion. Bruises & swollen state of knuckles gives impression argument physical in nature. As captain, my duty 2 record conditions of weather & crew, but wanted 2 put down in writing what I know about group joining us in case I put 1 or more ashore.

Clear horizon this day. Strong wind pushes us.

Octo de Nonus, a.CDXCIX

Wind blows S/SW & slows ship. Sky clear.

1 crewman sick. Another injured from skirmish that awoke me late into night. Skirmish related 2 gambling. Numeri, I think. Unable 2 learn name of assaulting party, but found Fortis unconscious reeking of wine. Hands bloodied. Claimed injuries from helping w/mast. Crewman substantiated claim yet I remain unconvinced.

Something wrong w/Fortis. Rather sturdy build & appears in good health so must B within whatever ails him. Rot not so different than what ruins harbor vessel left too long unattended.

Hope he does not cast clouds over voyage. Sizable profits await.

Novum de Nonus, a.CDXCIX

Have gone w/o sleep so will B brief. Last night I chose 2 keep eyne on nighttime happenings. No trouble. Either Fortis still suffers from injuries or sizable friend kept him confined. I guess latter.

Wind S/SW. Has picked up. Our speed ever sluggish.

Sick crewman's fever worsened. Fear red dots will appear on crewman's flesh.

Pray 2 Caeruleus the sea-god protect us as he does waters.

Decem de Nonus, a.CDXCIX

Wind now N/NE. Ship speedier.

Woman Jana (WJ) - healer - offered 2 help sick crewman. Diagnosis not bova (what I feared). When crew got word, crew worried if crewman caught illness from lupa in Dahak. WJ ensured not due 2 severity of crewman's symptoms. His disease not catching w/o contact of sexual nature. Morbus gallicus. Late stages. Sick man prone 2 outbursts rife w/insanity. Unclear how effective WJ treatments will B. We lack 3 of the necessary herbs & affliction something he has had long time.

Wonder if same disease infects Fortis & has not shown every trait as of yet. At times his ramblings are like crewman's. WJ claims Fortis's outbursts come from drink & sorrow.

Undecim de Nonus, a.CDXCIX

Wind remains N/NE. Strong. Ship speed great.

Crewman's condition worsens despite WJ's remedies. His madness unnerves crew reluctant 2 believe her reassurances. Think his illness prophetic, punishment handed down by Caeruleus. Only blood sacrifice will calm great god, crew say.

Stationed 2 crewmen as guards. Sick man now resides in my quarters.

Deuodecim de Nonus, a.CDXCIX

Small uprising among crew. 2 guards insufficient protection 4 crewman. Guards dropped swords at 1st sign of trouble. W/my own eyne, I saw this and thought party of 4 would kill sick crewman. Then what seemed a demon erupted from bows of ship 2 foil attack. Could sight nothing more than silver streaks of mucrones he wielded. 2 crewmen dead. Fortis obviously drunk. Stumbled back 2 depths from whence came.

Sick crewman lives. Each breath owed 2 Fortis.

Have oft heard tale of demens bellatores & how these warriors become mad w/rage. Mayhap Fortis is of different sort & much better swordsman drunk than sober. Either way, I owe man debt.

Uneven but strong wind blows W.

Tredecim de Nonus, a.CDXCIX

Events of day have forced me 2 wait B4 writing log. Fortis came after sunrise w/WJ. Assisted in caring 4 ill. Sober throughout morning & afternoon. Evening as well. Apologized 4 being disruption. I am left clueless as 2 reason 4 his new humility. Easy 2 C humbleness does not suit him.

Crewman is getting no better & fares no worse. Recovery would B good 4 crew as grumblings of us having offended Caeruleus continue. Cannot afford more fighting and losing men.

Wind W. Has picked up. Rain threatens.

Note. Passed Sanguinem Insula. Has been uninhabited 4 generations yet ship anchored & tender left ashore. Odd. Must make inquiries. No persons in right minds visit forsaken spot.

Quattuordecim de Nonus, a.CDXCIX

2-day we gave sea our sick crewman. May Caeruleus watch over him in deep waters. Fortis surprised me. Spoke eloquently of death & pain of folk left behind. Good 2 know Fortis not always barbarus.

Note. Certain familiarity between Fortis & WJ. Am ignorant 2 whether relationship is intimate. Mayhap this is Y he is serener.

Arranged 4 gambling 2 lighten crew's mood.

Strong wind again at our backs. Waves break B4 us.

Quindecim de Nonus, a.CDXCIX

1 crewman dead. Sword through gut. 2 others injured. Mistaken about Fortis. Pure animal him. He is shackled & will remain so 4 rest of journey. Will have Floridus arrested—

WJ just visited my quarters. Informed me no uncertain terms proconsul would halt any prosecution of Fortis. Has also informed me crew whispers of taking revenge on Fortis. WJ says should any attempt on man's life prove successful, my own would B forfeit.

Caeruleus, how _do_ I get into these situations?

XII

VERMIS

During days upon days so nondescript Indrasena lost track of how many passed she came to understand the purpose of the gray-skin witchcraft; that their chants and smoke brought her closer in mind and spirit to the bimembrae. Always ensuing the spell a gray-skin repeated his demand she eat while he tossed into the pit another heart. Several laid strewn about, the oldest festering whereas the freshest leaked blood heavy rain was washing away.

The storm she thought of as good and bad. Good for cleansing the air of stench and providing a greater amount of water than what the plagiariae gave—just enough to keep her alive—but the ground would dry slow and she would be colder than before, confronted with the type of chill that penetrated her bones. Still, the rain cleaned off her grime and the water filling the holes she dug might see her through a week or two. Among the strongest of her hopes regarding the water was that the tall mud-banks she built around the wells kept out the tallow, wormy creatures that came after the first heart began rotting. The creatures fed off it and others using tiny sharp teeth. Indrasena knew of the teeth since a few infantile vermes had worked their way into the gash starting at the corner of her mouth and stopping where a sideburn would grow were a cock dangling between her legs. Revolting, how the worms squirming made her cheek twitch. Painful, too, those nips the vermes took of her wound, the result of her landing on a rock in yet another failed escape, the same rock she earlier uncovered and tried to dislodge for a weapon.

Laughable idea.

She did not possess the strength for wielding an object similar to a cannonball and lacked an extra hand to take it with her when trying to scale the pit. Funny how despair and anguish and wretchedness granted the near-dying unfound strength and stupidity. Even had she climbed outside, there was nowhere to go. This on top of being no match for the stronger gray-skins and incapable of outrunning the nimble plagiariae.

None of that lucidness, however, mattered. What did? Her getting *outside*. She wanted more than anything for her dying breath to be without the odors of dirt, rock, mildew, and decomposing animal parts, to be without—

She winced and picked at a vermis burrowing nearest her mouth. The slick, vile, squidgy worm kept slipping from her fingers swollen and abraded after her climbing and digging the holes, tearing off several nails in her efforts.

If she employed patience, ceased wincing, stayed calm, pinched gentle...

The tiny vermis she held writhed and half-encircled her forefinger, its biting her an act of self-defense given the creatures ate exposed flesh and preferred the putrid kind. The latter they went after in relentless fashion. No dormancy for them. When not eating, they mated at an alarming rate. Grew quick, too. The largest out there—the length of her hand and wrist—originally measured smaller than the one she held that went limp and drooped.

Did it play dead?

The clever little thing wriggled as she squeezed. How had it learnt such a trick? She licked her lips, surprised by the severe pangs shooting through her gut and bewildered because her eating the vermes went unconsidered until now. She knew they were sources of food thanks to the lout who delivered wild beasts her father trained.

What had been the hunter's...had she called him by name? She shook her head—no, she used an epithet—never an imaginative child she—any nickname concocted by her imagination must have been simple, rather obvious.

Hunter-Man.

Whose carrot-colored hair went uncut and beard grew as wild. He lugged an axe and chuckled upon her asking what he ate out in the forests. Despite his bending to wink at her, his great height forced her to crane her neck so she could look at his pockmarked face—ugly that, but she maintained her gaze anyway since Pater insisted his children act polite and she loved pleasing her father.

"Me eats li'l worms," claimed Hunter-Man.

She recalled scrunching her nose, saying with a large measure of skepticism, "Worms?"

"Uh-huh. Sometimes me lucky. Find carcass part rotted. In them is worms. Grubs. How you say? Vermes." He straightened, patted his belly. "Take on carcass flav if got-to in time."

This vermis between her fingers then tasted of her cheek. She gazed past the wriggler at the vermes covering the bimembrorum hearts like slithering tendrils. If she partook of them, those she chose were to be off fresher meat. Not that big worm, either. Too disgusting due to its size, the way its juices might run down her chin and its entrails swamp her tongue. Smaller vermes, though; she imagined eating them no different than dining on raw ranunculae, those teeny soft-bodied fishes with tendril-tails Pater had taught her to cook.

"Salt them well, Indra," she remembered Pater saying, smiling.

Her admitting she would never again see the grin which caused folk to presume her father sarcastic wrought a pain severer than starvation. To keep from crying she dropped the grub and limped to the newest heart. No vermes on it. She squinted peering around the pit, trying to determine...so hard to tell which hearts were older in the dwindling light with everything wet, but maybe if she put her nose closer...

On hands-and-knees she went, her limbs shaking, to the next heart and sniffed in earnest. Once her retching passed, she hovered her face over another, except this time she took a smaller breath. Her luck needed to improve, else her arms and legs give up the hunt. The third—or fourth?—smelled fresher though not to the point she could eat it. Her reaching the fifth took longer, repeatedly pitching into the mud how she did. The sixth vermes-infested heart appeared less rank.

She opted for a grub colored brighter than its brothers and sisters and deposited it in her mouth. Indrasena chewed what was squishy, bitter; somewhat sour with a meaty flavor. In her fumbling for another, other vermes tried to latch onto her. Fast they moved. She jerked back and stood. Thinking of how the vermis she plucked from her cheek played dead, she wondered whether these attempted to defend their own kind, but no worms or snakes she ever heard of presented a pack mentality. She bent and picked a vermis alone and on the edge of the heart, then plopped it into her mouth and spat it out amid loosing a shrill scream. She kicked with her right leg to get her ankle away from the monster masticating it.

The large vermis she had judged too disgusting to eat slithered to her left, opened its mouth wide. Serrated teeth snapped shut on her foot. She screeched, lurched forth, stumbled, flailed at nothing, was falling. Face-first into the mud. Tiny, tallow bodies covered her arms, slithered up her sides. Her thighs and calves were on fire. She crawled on her belly, crying and babbling, halted and beat at those worms on her back; this before flipping and flopping as a fish did on a riverbank and slapping at those parasites writhing along her stomach and stinging her genitals.

From overhead came flashes of someone large leaping into the pit and cursing in an incomprehensible tongue. She was whisked up and flung like a sack. It was then, when her gut hit the gray-skin's shoulder, that the air rushed from her and she fainted.

XIII

FLORIDUS

Were there music to what felt like awakening from the dead, Caderyn supposed those notes would come from out-of-tune strings and cacophonic drumming. Not that the groan-inducing twangs and thumping in his head brought about the most unpleasant of sensations; no, that honor went to the utter darkness giving him a sense of weightlessness that soured his gut. Before the forbearer of vomit burning his throat spoiled his tongue, he sat up to stand, getting no farther than sliding to the side of the bed and resting his elbows on his knees. He let his head dangle, contemplated wiping away the spittle wetting his chin, decided the effort was monumental, and wondered if he had contracted an illness. In all probability what he suffered was a wicked hangover. Or perhaps his overwhelming desire to dispel whatever poisoned his stomach was...

Not due to the ship.

His feet were planted on blessed, cool, unforgiving stone rather than on waterlogged planks that creaked and bowed. Gone was the damnable and overwhelming yet subtle odor of brine seeping into his clothes, hair, and skin. Absent, too, were the pongs of unwashed crewmen. In their steads came the fragrances of pine trees and—he grimaced, recognizing the flower that served as the base for Elianna's perfume.

Sweet alyssum.

Mountainous bouquets of white petals, green and yellow centers. He was on land, assumed this home to be the villa of

Proconsul Lepidus. Caderyn leaned forward and paused while gathering the will to rise. He did so in the manner of a decrepit old man, his joints popping like a fire crackled, and swayed as a sapling caught in a healthy crosswind until his wobbly knees deposited him back onto the bed, palms pressing against a damp mattress.

Damp, why damp?

Short of breath, he rubbed his chest. Dowsed. Sick then; yes, he had been sick and whatever fever that infected him had broken. Odd he did not recall coming down with anything. What he last remembered was enjoying Derigo, a game the captain suggested that Caderyn and crewmen swapped turns playing. The game-board was an indented wheel, the indentations along the four spokes and in the wheel's center holding-places for game-balls. One player received a set of three black, the other player white. Whomever put their balls in a line first was the victor. Maneuvers were difficult, jumping game-pieces over those of an opponent prohibited. Many times Caderyn had lost before developing a good strategy. Accusations of him cheating led to a fight which ended when immense pain erupted at the crown of his skull and blackness plagued him.

Oblivion.

Nice that, devoid of drunkenness, self-loathing, and obsessing over Elianna, their marriage, his asinine refusal to accept her death and start anew, something Jana had...?

Jana...

Cold fingers walked up his spine. Why the sudden guilt? Had they...? He rubbed his eyes, strained to recall...*anything*...and got impressions of anger, fear, fighting, reheard laughter as intoxicating as beer and wine, echoes of moans in the dark, memory-glimpsed lips and bared skin, heard again cursing and frustration before his loyalty to a deceased wife washed away the partial recollections.

He reconsidered rising and getting the investigation he almost quit started, find some purpose, a reason to continue breathing, but really, the only thing he wanted to do was retreat to the Land of Nil. Bow to Death and summon peace. Obtain serenity once and forever. But then if he were to do that, he needed...

Where *were* his weapons? Clothes? Whose was this room he occupied, its lamps and the materials to ignite them?

Questions, riddles, running down answers and chasing resolutions. Futile. Naught was ever known or settled. Why, why did he stay stuck in this nowhere place of indecision, of bouncing back and forth between a wonderful past and horrid present?

A man ignorant of his true spirit was no man at all, so maybe he had always been a boy pretending at adulthood. Nothing else explained how a nobilis celebrated surrendered to mediocrity, who sat inside a rich man's home with a cracked skull entertaining suicidal notions, feeling set adrift within this strange room to where he had been hauled and remained unconscious until...

What hour was it?

Night—obvious—but few places were without a shred of light. There were doorways, windows should this be a modern villa. He stared straight ahead while keeping his eyes unfocused.

Forms took on vague shapes. To his right was an arched outline. Access to a wardrobe? Curtains draped an entryway in front of him. The exit, he supposed, to a common-room, almost certainly the atrium given that out there moonlight shone. He twisted to look behind him. Pitch black. Off to his left were vertical lines of moonlight glowing through the cracks of what he deemed a shutter. He and Elianna had purchased similar items for their own villa, she insistent on the matter seeing how these shutters were excellent at providing darkness. He had been eager to oblige. Anything to keep her happy. Anything except staying sober and becoming the man she loved. Would he fail Indrasena as well, leave her to whatever end because his miring in self-pity prevented him from saving her? For how many decades would the shame last of letting the woman die he swore to rescue?

Longer than letting the boy get raped.

Time. Whatever hour, it was time.

He stood on rickety legs and lumbered to the window, raised the shutter to look out at the swaying conical trees that formed a marked, dark line against the night-sky. The line of trees ran along crags of the mountains, making the world appear as if it ended. He turned. Looking inside the room was better, reassured him he was not about to go falling into the abyss.

Oil-lamps interspersed with robin-like shapes on the wall opposite him. Where had he heard about bird-patterns? A café, the Thermopolium de Calasade serving hot, tepid, and cellared refreshments. Birds had something to do with Jana's reply to his asking where Indrasena slept. He almost...not quite...he released the wisp that got wilder with his trying to tame it.

Between him and the flock stood the bed, a three-sided rectangular box with an open side for getting in and out and a roll-pillow that rested on a headboard slanting backwards and curving under at the top. The blanket soft and padded had decorative swirls sewn into it. A bowl on the nightstand stored jewelry. He rifled through the rings and necklaces, the majority inexpensive brass. A bracelet of twisting silver bands festooned in sapphires was worth a hefty sum. Curious, that co-existence of cheap and lavish. Somebody ascending to wealth would have gotten rid of the shoddier pieces whereas someone fallen on desperate times would sell the bracelet. Who kept both? What sort of person with whom Lepidus associated lived among neither the rank of slave nor master? A definite oddity; within the proconsul's world society etched the borders of social stratification in granite.

Likewise, roaming in the same nowhere territory, were the quarters he occupied. Furnished with a nightstand counting as the only adornment besides the bed, the room was empty for a noble and plush for a slave. Caderyn mulled the afternoon he and Jana met, remembering easily her chagrin over being prohibited from discussing any detail outside Indrasena's kidnapping.

"Mayhap," he mused, *"other reasons besides coin or politics fueled Indrasena's kidnapping. Is she beautiful?"*

Jana. *"You judge that upon seeing a painting of the—her."*

Which helped his recollecting Jana's reply to the inquiry of where Indrasena slept.

"Quarters accessing the atrium. A bedchamber. Private and prettier than most with its robin-decorated wall."

So they had boarded him in the girl's room—logical because it was vacant. What confused him was a painting commissioned in the likeness of a...What *was* she to the proconsul? Servant? Houseguest? Lover? Might then Lepidus insist artwork of her be kept someplace private yet viewable to his object of desire?

Caderyn ran his fingers along the front of the nightstand for the crevices of a drawer. He found none and crouched to search the stand's shelves and fumbled across flint, char-cloth, and steel. He used those to light the trio of oil-lamps on the wall. No art save for the robins. A nice illusion, though, their wings fluttering thanks to the flickering flames.

He considered the wardrobe. Foolish not to think of it before since a painting remained a secret kept as bad hanging in these chambers as out in the atrium.

Fueled by motivation, a little jubilated having *any* purpose, he parted the closet's lace curtains. Within were plain stolae, fibulae, and pallae. Well-worn and oft-washed, all retained stale mixtures of ammonia and vanilla. At the end of the clothes-rod, as if the person who stored the garment wished to hide it, he discovered a satin nightdress near transparent, saffron print. Another gift? Odorless, not faded. New or...? Were such presents unwanted, the girl would have set aside the bracelet instead of storing it with her other jewelry and discarded this nightdress to the floor or stuffed it someplace out-of-sight, out-of-mind. Lepidus's gifts were therefore coveted and thus, the nightdress was near new.

Caderyn rehung the gown and returned to the bed. He laid down, lacing his fingers behind his tender and bandaged head, and pondered the best way of approaching Lepidus. The proconsul was an accomplished man, wedded if typical of someone in his position, but politicians were no strangers to extramarital affairs either. The many allusions pointing at the man's emotional involvement with a woman other than his wife meant questioning him was tricky unless Caderyn wanted to estrange his best source for clues regarding who took the girl.

If she was taken.

No, an inane thought Indrasena's leaving of her own accord. In that case she would have taken the bracelet. Or... she was too bitter to bring it, having lain here night after night stewing over a man unable to come to her bed because of a jealous and suspicious wife. Stewing and staring at those robins, their illusionary flight, much like he did except with her there was no fear of nightmarish things.

Despite willing himself to do otherwise, he closed his eyes, drifted, slept in fitful spans, and reawakened midmorning to the scents of fresh-baked bread and Jana's perfume. For the first time he saw her dressed in garb other than a tunic and breeches and found he disliked the purple stola that concealed her breasts and the curves of her hips.

She put the platter of food on the nightstand. "You awoke last night?"

He sat up, nodded.

"Apologies." Her smile rose on one side, putting the cutest dimple in her cheek. "Know my absence was to hasten your physical recovery. Had I been present, well…"

His hand stopped midway to the food and hung aloft as he fought a renewed bout of queasiness. Had he bedded Jana? Dare he ask? Damn the blackouts. Misera, he thought, goddess of mercy, let this be not so.

"Are you dizzy?" Jana asked.

"I" —*Lie*— "Aio. Can I have something to drink?"

"Juice?"

He hoped his grin of approval was stronger than the expression felt.

"Eat the pear while I am away. It will be *moist,* like everything of a delicious nature."

Her words, her teasing, looking over her shoulder as she left; were those flirting? He gave his gut a chance to expel the butterflies and set about eating. She was right, in the end, about the pear's succulence. He moved on to the strawberries, consuming them with patience to give Jana more time to bring the juice for washing-down the fish that looked overcooked. When yet no sign of her came and Caderyn swallowed the final strawberry, he nibbled at the ends of what he believed was cod. He finished the fish and still, Jana stayed gone.

He waited, fidgeted, paced to-and-fro alongside the bed, thinking it unwise to go parading around Lepidus's villa searching for Jana dressed in a subligaculum that just concealed his groin and displayed his ass-cheeks. This hour of the day any proconsul attended to clients. In turning Caderyn spied beneath the bed the burnished hilts of his swords laying atop his clothes and chest harness. He hoped to find the painting of Indrasena under there, too.

As disappointing was the food's failure to restore his strength. After dressing and exiting Indrasena's cubiculum, he made it halfway across the atrium before resting, perching on the basin that captured and drained rainwater into wells beneath the house. He peered upward and gazed through the hole in the roof at a blue sky. The distance from that compluvium to where he sat was perhaps twice his height. A light kidnapper with cushioned soles could land unheard on the marble floor, but the jump needed to be at an angle for the kidnapper to eschew the pool. Likelier the plagiarius slid down a rope, then swung between the four corner columns of the impluvium to alight inside the atrium, the room for receiving and impressing visitors, which this did with the largest and tiniest of details.

Smaller aspects included the impluvium masked in tangerine and black mosaics. Caderyn swishing the water revealed gold specks embedded in those tiles. The largest details comprised works of art covering the atrium's walls.

One mural featured a cloud-enshrouded mountain, the second a beach at high tide. The third presented a woman of breath-stealing beauty with supple features, flowing chestnut hair. Her steel-gray irises peppered in amber dots harbored a surprising real-life quality. Incongruous, those eyes; how they spoke of ages past while the woman's complexion glistened yesterday's newness. The painting was idealized—had to be with her lack of pores, wrinkles, and blemishes. Since funeral masks of Lepidus's ancestors rested on shelving above her head, Caderyn guessed the woman to be the familia matriarch.

Through no small amount of effort he swept his stare to the other side of the room and settled it on an artistic representation of the Bleeding Grounds. The arena was oval in shape, exterior plastered in limestone reflecting the rays of a sun unseen, and dwarfed the city beside it. If true-to-life, the stadium seated ten times more people than the several thousand of a normal-sized quadratum. Fittingly in front of the Bleeding Grounds' mural was a delubrum, a small chapel for hosts and guests to honor the deceased by kneeling and placing a left palm over their heart.

Murmurs drew his attention.

Through a corridor to his right Caderyn saw the office area—the tablinum—and beyond that, the plush garden of the peristylium three people exited. Jana and Proconsul Lepidus strolled on either side of a man wearing an orange toga. Once the trio entered the tablinum, the proconsul and the man grasped each other's forearms in a handshake signifying an official agreement had been reached. Tradition that and the same dictated Lepidus walk out his client. If the proconsul saw Caderyn, he might request a meeting for which Caderyn was unprepared.

He rose and went through the passage exiting the house, stepping around the miniature bed-statue symbolizing the sanctity of marriage that confirmed his suspicions of Lepidus's marital status.

Outside he drew an extensive breath—the day warm, the breeze a welcomed caress—listening to the chirping of birds sitting in trees on the outskirts of the expansive grounds. He scratched his cheek, thinking a shave was overdue, and remembered sitting across from Jana at the Thermopolium and asking her what happened to Indrasena.

"...vanished in the middle of the night. We were unaware of her missing until the next morning when she did not show up for breakfast. Once the proconsul's hysterics ended, we searched the villa and its immediate grounds. We discovered a ladder on the atrium's roof..."

During the war, following Caderyn's legion advancing into Permia and mountainous terrain, the general Ducis Alexander had assigned Caderyn nocturnal look-out duties. On clear nights the mountains grew little darker than murky dawns. Lepidus's trees were a couple hundred yards from the villa, the distance considerable for kidnappers carrying a ladder. Caderyn had to assume those who possessed the wits to sidestep the peristylium would not hazard running in the open hauling a large object. They would have awaited cloud-cover and camped far enough to escape notice but close enough to watch the villa, biding their time for days or weeks of summer when the rainy season had ended. A long stay; a source of signs to who they were and hints of where they...

Where *could* they have fled after nabbing the girl?

Caderyn stepped off the porch and walked between wheel-dug trenches to the edge of the C-shaped plateau on which the villa was built. He trailed his eyes along the wending, downward road to where metal glinted. From that, expanding in either direction and passing through the trees, was a protective wall ending at mountainsides. How many men would clever plagiariae have used when they needed to circumvent a guarded gate? Less than a handful for sneaking through while a guard pissed or shat. These particular escapists would have been hampered by taking a young woman—light, but...lugging her that distance...a very strong man. Two people. One nimble and thin to sneak inside the villa, the other an oxen to haul them out and...

Carry Indrasena those long miles? Ample opportunity for her to put up a struggle or raise an alarm. Brash and fatuous were not attributes of plagiariae intelligent and patient. Even had they drugged the girl or knocked her out, the complication of distracting those manning the gate or scaling a tall fortification remained. After that, a strenuous hike out of mountains at least somewhat populated.

An improbable way to flee.

If they fled.

Caderyn turned around. His vantage point at the rim of the crag-sided horseshoe containing Lepidus's villa gave him a better view of the outlying forest-area. The half-circle expanse to where inclines led to crags was searchable. Combing the woods could uncover signs of a camp and what was left of a ravaged woman's corpse—gnawed bones scattered among the remnant strips of a nightdress befitting a slave that in actuality a lover had donned.

An illicit affair.

What motive to suppress your messenger and offer a colossal reward.

Mayhap, he thought, aware his breathing had quickened and his body coursed with vitality, the proconsul's wife discovered her husband's indiscretion. Jealousy was a fine reason for killing.

By the gods, if he were to never toil in boredom, he might never again get drunk. He was flying now, a winged predator gliding, seeking a morsel, prepared to swoop upon spotting it. His feet charging forward were the hooves of a battle-frenzied stallion and his mind a honed knife slicing away a mystery crust to expose clues underneath. Clues such as the indentations on the villa's silver-leaf gutter and subtle depressions in the ground along the eastern side of the house. A ladder placed there that someone heavy climbed?

He glared at the woods, trying to penetrate them. A search was definitely in order. Expand the scope if he uncovered nothing until he flung back the blanket, and what then?

Drink, gamble?

Find the killers.

Then?

Drink—

"Apologies," Jana said, standing at the villa's corner, "for failing to deliver your juice. Lepidus demanded a woman's sensibilities for bringing about a satisfactory end to a client-meeting." She gave a leering smile identical to her earlier offering. "Your color has returned."

He pointed upward at the sun. "Clupeus blazes this day."

"I was unaware you believed in the gods." The crossing of her arms emphasized her cleavage revealed by a tighter-fitting robe than what she wore previous.

Was his envisioning caressing her breasts memory or fantasy? "My faith runs along the same wavering lines as my sobriety."

"What" —she drew beside him— "is consistent about you?"

He concentrated on her freckles to elude her eyes and diffuse the energy between them. Her standing this close, he could get caught up in her stare, go adrift on the wafts of her perfume familiar and foreign all at once. He wanted to kiss her. Had he already? At some juncture during his musing, his hand acquired its own will and went to rest on the small of Jana's back. He pulled it away.

"I see," she said, her voice revealing no emotion. "Are we to continue dancing hither-thither, or might you stumble the road home?"

Stumble the road home; was that her way of saying she wanted...?

Focus. "This eve I will meet with Mathis and Jacob prior to the proconsul."

"Infeasible. Your friends went to question the servae about Indrasena's vanishing despite Lepidus's assurances they told everything they know."

"When?"

"Two days ago."

Two days...

Jana snickered. "I can see you estimating their return in the wrinkling of your forehead. Over a hundred servae tend the cherry trees in a valley halfway down these mountains. Jacob and Mathis may yet be gone awhile."

"Send someone to fetch them. Better they help me search the nearby woods."

She curtsied, giggling. "Exquisitor. Your will, my hands." Her titter escalated into full laughter.

"Why the joviality?"

Jana coughed as her gaiety died, her cheeks now rose-tinted. "No matter. A joke that reflected on our journey together should not be so private only one of us enjoys it. How many extra people to aid your search?"

"None."

"You suspect the servae?"

"And anyone else able to come and go from the villa without raising suspicion."

"Including me?"

He met her gaze, stared straight into her eyes. Lovely skin and lips added to tempting curves did not equate to innocence. "My job is to stay sober and rescue Indrasena. To that end I must remain unbiased."

"Quite a quick turnaround. Without Jacob forcing you to come or my holding your hand aboard ship, you would lay dead or so drunk you may as well be."

He swung his gaze to the ground, her sandaled feet. "I was— uh, idleness is—" Her painted toes, how would she react were he to suck on them? "I...ruminate. During darker times my tendency is to succumb...Your tone has turned harsh. Have I hurt you?"

"Hurt? Naught of that sort."

The question, "Have I bedded you?" pushed for voice. In addition to the embarrassment of having to ask, there was the propensity of learning he had been inside a woman other than his wife. The guilt of that had the potential to send him down the spiral staircase. Smarter evading cataclysmic subjects.

Caderyn nodded to himself. "We should learn whether any townspeople recall sighting Indrasena the night of her disappearance. While in Polus you mentioned a painting of her I thought to show around Floridus."

Her laugh was acrimonious. "Should your arms stretch wide enough."

"What do you mean?"

"Verum," she seethed, "I had no idea your obtuseness was this thick. Figure it out. When you do, invite the townsfolk to the villa. Line them up single-file starting at the atrium and continuing on the lawn and down the road. Charge admission. People would pay were the *art's* sheer lewd size advertised. Were her beauty. Or why *he* had the painting created. Let each customer admire its excruciating detail and marvel as I did and do and must and witnessed *you* doing the same. You will have more chance of shining light on someone's recollection should their memories have darkened. *Which* I rather doubt. Nobody could forget seeing *her*."

In the wake of such vehemence, he stood like a simpleton with his jaw dropping while he sought to calm churning thoughts. Why was she so jealous? Did she want Lepidus and he had spurned her for a younger, prettier woman?

The gods as his witnesses, Caderyn wanted to shout at Jana, repeat over and over until his shouting sunk in how beautiful she was in her own right, how special. Proud and independent. Fearless. Honorable. Seductive and attractive in ways only surviving trials wrought. She was complex, had depth that went beyond the surface of her skin and the curves of her body, though those were lovely enough and...

"Caderyn, you blush."

"The..." He put his hand to his mouth and cleared his throat. "Heat, aio. The artist who painted Indrasena's mural, is he in Floridus?"

"Query Lepidus. In the tablinum."

"Jana..." He reached for her arm.

"Dare not touch me unless the touch leads to intimacy."

His hand dropped.

"I see," she muttered. "It is the dance of hither-thither. Go. Just...*go*."

XIV

MURALIS

To linger meant succumbing to his ache for caressing Jana, so Caderyn obeyed her command and went. Labored rather. Fatigue seeped into his legs as he slipped inside the villa's door ajar. When he entered the atrium, he stared at Indrasena's bedchamber, musing on the bed's comfort and ignoring the murals since the last thing he needed in light of his conflicted emotions was to gaze upon paintings of the Bleeding Grounds and Lepidus's stunning familia matriarch.

Or—his walking slowed—was this...?

"Is she beautiful?"

"You judge that upon seeing..."

He halted at the impluvium's midway point, gazed across the pool reflecting the afternoon sun, was again dumbstruck by the woman's exoticness, her pronounced cheekbones, the feral chestnut hair side-parted, her eyebrows a shade darker—the variance in tint expressed a love for the sun—her lashes thick and long, symmetrical eyes in the shapes of almonds. Those lips that any man would fall on his knees in begging to kiss showed pristine teeth. Quite a mischievous grin with the subtle crookedness— what thoughts *did* she entertain while the painter stroked his brush? Her jawline wide at the back angled to a rounded chin hanging low over a lithe neck, throat finely detailed. A deep dimple rested between her clavicle bones. There was not enough space to tell whether she had been nude at the time of her posing because the painting ended at the floor, cutting off at the swells of her breasts.

"...marvel as I did and do and must and witnessed you doing the same..."

Indrasena.

What drove a married man to commission an artist to do this then put the art in view of everyone? A harsh slap in the face to any wife, the painting residing in the same room as the lectus genialis. Was divorce an explanation for why he had not seen the house's domina and the reason Lepidus called on Jana to end a client-meeting?

A woman's sensibilities...

He bit his bottom lip, hoping Jana kept his head injury and drunken stupors from the proconsul and thereby maintained Lepidus's faith most people dared not store in a downtrodden, former nobilis. The ever-present desire for drink worsening, Caderyn willed away his rising hand.

No, no wiping or buckling, not this quick after surviving another storm. Later maybe. Probably. Inevitably.

But *not* now.

Head down, bulling onward, he walked through a pair of open folding doors to the tablinum. Marble walls of deep blue were sectioned off in three crimson panels outlined in thin strips of white and thicker swipes of broader turquoise. The proconsul reclined on a daybed situated against the far wall in-line with opposing windows filtering sunlight. His back rested against a padded end of the lectus, right arm outstretched along the furniture's spine. He had laid his other across a wooden pedestal beside the daybed, the fingers of his left hand dangling and spinning a cherry by its stem over a bowl full of fruit.

Lepidus glared straight ahead away from Caderyn. "Ah, the wayward exquisitor appears. How does his injury fare?"

Not the warm greeting he had wanted and one which introduced a flutter in his chest. That word again. *Exquisitor*. Had Jana told the proconsul whichever story made her giggle?

Caderyn sat in one of the two wicker chairs facing the lectus. "My head heals. Enough that I formulate plans."

"And what of Indrasena's disappearance? Any cogitations towards that end?"

He looked to the glass decanter filled with water sitting atop the pedestal and swallowed, his gullet dry. "Is the porta of your estate always guarded?"

"Day and night, for my political status brings many enemies." Lepidus spoke in a voice livelier than before, nose raised in a haughty manner. "Two or more custodes guard the gate at any given time. Barracks are within shouting distance and house a dozen men."

Then no, Caderyn reasoned, no feasible way the plagiariae escaped that route unless— "Any possibility your custodes accept bribes?"

"Insomuch as they cease valuing their lives and those of their wives and children."

Caderyn rubbed his neck. "I am unsure whether you would appreciate my theory. You were...close, shall we say—to Indrasena."

"Close?" Lepidus moved his jaw side-to-side, his temple bulging, as he bobbed the cherry. "What gives you this impression? The mural?"

"That. The silver bracelet festooned in sapphires. A silk nightdress with saffron print hanging inside Indrasena's wardrobe. I suspected she put the gown to the side because it was unimportant to her. Now I imagine its position means she wanted to keep it out-of-sight. Secrecy denotes intimacy."

Lepidus cocked his head, daylight shining through the windows gleaming on his bald crown. "You have been awake so short a time yet managed a good bit of investigative work. Impressive."

Caderyn waited, expecting Lepidus to append for a drunkard.

The proconsul did not. "Forget the relationship I have with *my* ancilla."

Ancilla, body slave. Indrasena had then tended to Lepidus's attire, cleansed him, fed him; whatever duty fell within the realm of personal nature. Caderyn got up. He reached for the glass decanter of water, took a long drink. Before retaking his seat, he nabbed a cherry and ate it.

"Sweeter and tarter than any lowland fruit," Lepidus claimed. "I owe them my fortune for the wine they create."

"It is my understanding grapes, not cherries, are used for vinum."

"Any fruit can produce wine. In mine, grapes play a part during fermentation. Afterwards, too, when their juice is reduced to defrutum. The rest of the recipe I shall keep to not have you competing with me courtesy the money I pay you." The proconsul's smile was more smirk than grin. "What do you believe happened to Indrasena?"

Since the man yearned for honesty... "She lies dead somewhere in the forest. I stand convinced no one could have carried her away without notice. As to motive for her murder. You are an important man in a powerful position and angered the wrong person. Her death was their revenge."

"I see." What followed was as curt. "You are an assumptive fool. No one knew of Indrasena's importance. Is not their business. At least not yet."

"Care to tell me?"

Lepidus set his lips firm and continued staring frontward.

Caderyn sighed. "How can I rescue the girl if you hide things about her from me?"

"Limit your concerns to her vanishing. It is all that matters."

Caderyn pressed his tongue to the roof of his mouth, yet his tongue refused to stay still. "Why have the mural created?"

"Rein in your insolence."

"But surely your wife objected to—"

"Which has *naught* to do with Indrasena getting stolen from my domus."

"Lepidus, I cannot identify suspects ignorant of why she might have—"

"Forget might. She *was* taken. Our window for rescuing her closes with each passing hour."

"Any suspects—?"

"You are to ferret those. Best start earning the fortune offered afore I renege and hire someone more willing to find actual evidence."

Which perchance was a corpse. "I will first search the woods."

Lepidus rolled his eyes. "We combed that area *twice* thinking the felons hid there."

"You looked for people whereas I will seek signs of them. A critical distinction. In the meantime I insist you commission an artist to paint three small replicas of Indrasena's mural."

"For what purpose?"

"One for me, another for Mathis, the last for Jacob. We will show them to townsfolk in the hopes we pinpoint someone who saw her and her captors."

"You waste what precious time may remain to Indrasena by re-canvasing the woods and trying to pick out a witness from some eight thousand people."

"The search is not so blind. This girl is memorable. No man with blood running in his veins soon forgets her. Neither does a woman with an ounce of envy. After investigating the woods, should I discover naught, I will visit local ports while Mathis and Jacob go to inns here and in neighboring towns. No demand for ransom tells us the plagiariae have objectives other than money. In such case why keep Indrasena in the vicinity of Floridus? They traveled somewhere and there are witnesses to that."

Again, Lepidus plopped a cherry into his mouth, chewed, gulped, and toyed with another piece of fruit. "You will need someone familiar with the city. Jana can serve as your guide."

"I am unsure she wants—"

"*That* is unimportant. She will do as commanded irrespective how she feels. Of the local ports there is but one. The dock's operarius is Judoc. Tall and skinny, shaggy hair colored black, tanned skin, piggish face." As Caderyn nodded and rose, the proconsul talked faster. "Jana informed me of what transpired during your trip here. Did the captain who bludgeoned you also confiscate your coin?"

"Aio."

Lepidus groped inside the folds of his brown tunica, jostling the sun emblem pinned at his shoulder that glinted upon getting moved. He brought out a pouch and dropped it onto the pedestal. "I presume this coin is less than the sum stolen but sufficient for you to compel Judoc to converse and your men to travel."

At last he looked at Caderyn. "Rest, exquisitor. You appear worn."

XV

ПOCTURПIS

Caderyn napped and awoke refreshed. After gobbling the food left for him on the nightstand, he meandered the villa eerie in its quietness, most occupants having retired for the night, and was careful to avoid tripping over the occasional sleeping slave. He ended up in the peristylium sitting on a bench, entertaining dismal hopes Jana appeared while regretting his ignorance of which cubiculum was hers or whether Mathis and Jacob had returned.

A discomforting thing uninformed of so much.

He shifted in his seat to find a comfortable spot for passing the hours as he watched night clouds drift in and out, some remaining and blotting the sky, their centers angry-looking, sinuous edges glowing purplish blue.

Nature's Art.

As a soldier he had not realized the serenity that mountains emitted because appreciating tranquility was impossible trudging terrain wet and miserable, so terrified that fear pained your bones like the cold. Upon his reflecting on the misery of living in Polus and before that—the war—he found he missed the mountains as they existed during those rare moments absent threat of losing or taking life, when he could breathe easy the crisp and thin air which expanded from his chest and seeped relaxation into his limbs.

A therapeutic area to settle this. Oh, he might not afford a homestead matching the prestige of what the proconsul owned, but the coin Lepidus paid could purchase a villa smaller though not too divergent. The cherries were a must. To eat, no vineyards. Ranch cattle for a living. People considered beef still new to Calasade a delicacy. A profitable enterprise.

The ground darkened to his right, Jacob's moonlight-born shadow portending the big man's arrival and preceding his baritone voice. "Here our leader is at last, awakened to the world and all it proffers superior to my dear colluvio." He plopped onto the bench to the sound of stone grinding. "The eye looks but it is the mind which sees. Do tell. What is in the Afterlife besides the astrum?"

"Mystery," Caderyn replied, "for erudition belongs to the gods and those rewarded after death. We among the living with innocence to lose fear enlightenment spiritual or otherwise." He traced his gaze along the top of the peristylium wall. "I have put this off for too long and asking you is easier than Jana. What happened between her and me aboard ship?"

Jacob smiled a little, a thin coat of awkwardness overlaying his amusement. "We learn not for the sake of wisdom but to prepare for life." Or did he grin with regret? "Not each proverb rings true. For instance one who asks shall never err."

"You will not say what transpired between her and me?"

"I am ignorant to that."

"Yet the wariness in your voice and mien hint you spotted things."

"Ah." Jacob crossed his arms. "Here is where you misstep. If I tell what I saw, you will draw conclusions. Assumptions will cause guilt. That is your grandest excuse for drinking."

"Whenever have I stumbled so quick upon regaining my feet?"

"Neither have you bedded a woman besides Elianna. Your devotion to her is what keeps you sober...part of the time and...what drives you to drink the rest. Best to protect what keeps you standing while it does and heed the teachings from the Keepers of Knowledge. 'Expose the foundation and the building shall crumble'."

Caderyn drummed his fingers on his thighs, contemplating words for maintaining the philosophical tone of their conversation. "My bridge to sobriety may yet collapse if denied proper maintenance. To wonder is unsettling and frays my trusses."

A whistle accompanied Jacob exhaling through his nose, his mouth closed tight. "The two of you held hands. I spied you kissing once. A peck. Innocent by the looks. An evening or three, you took walks along the railing and gazed out on the sea. During the daytime Jana was a constant at your side following a night you spent together in the cabin at the stern. Whether you could fututio drunk as you were" —he shrugged— "only the gods and Jana can say and the gods are forever silent. You must gather the courage to ask her." Jacob rose. It was as if the bench sighed. "For what reason did you summon me and Mathis?"

"Come sunrise we begin searching the woods. Lepidus thinks we do so for signs of a camp, but we also look for a corpse." He almost did not bother asking whether the servae had revealed consequential information, troubled as he was. There were times of stupor with Elianna he could not perform whereas others his cock rose to full-mast. His memories were hazy, built more on her statements than his own recollections. "Did you two discover anything?"

"When the custodes were present, nulla, not a peep worth reuttering, but between checks of the guard we pilfered tidbits. Indrasena was Lepidus's ancilla."

"This I knew."

Jacob bowed his head. "No small feat getting the proconsul to admit as much. Are you privy to her being the daughter of a beast-master?"

"You are saying she is a magum bestia?"

"Mayhap. Mental ability to control animals is not always inherited. What I can report with certainty is her father's sorcery withered. He turned to her brother and the brother was a failure. This is why Indrasena's familia defaulted on debts and fell into servitude. Many servae believe she is magum incarnate. Look at the dots in her eyne, they say. Amber signifies power." Jacob rocked foot-to-foot. "About Jana and your relationship—"

"I am aware of the advice you would counsel and recognize its logic, yet—"

"One's heart is stronger than the mind."

Caderyn nodded.

"Do not bother seeking drink. Lepidus put it under lock-and-key afore our arrival."

"She-bag, you fret for naught. My storm lies dormant for now. Which cubiculum is...?" He trailed off, scanning doorway-recesses.

"Jana retired after I did the one night Mathis and me stayed here." He expelled a heavy breath. "May dawn enlighten us come the morrow."

With Jacob vanishing down the corridor behind the tablinum, Caderyn went to the atrium. He took flint, char-cloth, and steel from the delubrum and lit the candled sconces peppered along the walls.

Light flickered across Indrasena's mural. He stared at her for a long time, cogitating his scant intelligence on magic. Legend disclosed that paranormal abilities in Calasade faded with each generation carrying his race, the Regna, farther from their ancestors, the Unayela, each of whom bore golden irises. It was said the gods intended for Regna to be feeble after a Unayelorum rebellion to topple the gods near succeeded. Regardless the narrative's historical accuracy, what could not be debated was that for untold generations no person sported amber eyes. At least no one noteworthy. Maybe in the far-off forests. There were instances, however, when a Regnum honed nuggets of power, their vigor reflected by the yellowy dots in their pupils. These folk often got conscripted into the military. A few were slain for fear of what havoc they might create.

Were her painting accurate, Indrasena harbored great potential and the ability to inspire mass after mass of seeing not just a woman compete—that alone was unprecedented—but witness one so exotic as she commanding beasts, her feminine beauty and sexuality a perfect counterbalance to barbaric, masculine violence. Should she become a callback to Regina de Arenae, the original Queen of the Sands, the proconsul need never worry over popularity. Little wonder then Lepidus had cloaked her true purpose by using her in a slave's capacity. A precious jewel she swimming in a sea of political sharks looking to gain the slightest advantage.

There was no curiosity either to Lepidus's refusal of confiding in the investigator he hired. Caderyn would have stayed in his homeland irrespective the coin offered had he known in the beginning his task was aiding the Bleeding Grounds. The proconsul without a doubt suspected this based on their first conversation within the Twisted Vine.

Perching on the edge of the impluvium, Caderyn flicked the pool's glasslike surface. Tiny waves undulated outward, languished, died. Another flick, harder this time as he pondered how to gain the upper hand, how to query his employer concerning other politicians without revealing his learning of Indrasena's true worth.

Flick.

While policing the streets of Polus, he had interrogated folk secretive and forthcoming, but nary one controlled the interview. Strategy and superiority provided the effectiveness to any investigation.

Lepidus...

"Verum, you wish to forgo a game? You ogle Imperatori as a forlorn lover might the woman gone from his embrace for a decade."

"It has not been so long."

"Three years then?"

Treacherous facing puissant opposition better informed of him than he was of it.

Caderyn sipped from his palm and wished for beer. Later, tucked away in Indrasena's bed and trying for a couple hours of fitful rest, he believed the blonde woman clad in a flimsy nightdress to be Elianna—that she and the perfume he smelled were out of a dream until realizing Jana stood over him. He prayed she go away.

She did.

After several minutes in which she sighed at intervals and altered her stance.

XVI

PRAEDATOR

Constant dripping. Drop after drop leaked through the tent's roof and spattered inside a tin pail on the floor that had been fascinating when Indrasena first came-to an hour or so ago. The floor was wood, good and solid, with the occasional knot. No dirt or mud or hearts.

Or vermes.

If not for the comfort of that and recent horrors, perhaps the leather strap going around and biting into her waist would have petrified her. Whatever buckle secured the belt was on the table's underside. To reach there was impossible, but even had she possessed the eight boneless and sucker-filled arms of an ocean-dwelling polypus, did the plagiariae and gray-skins deem her capable of fleeing? The simple labor of rising on her elbows made her pant like a rabid dog.

Everything summed up, tethered here was better than in the pit. The view was the lone exception. Through the tent's rectangular opening she saw gray-skins and numerous campfires going in a straight line until the dancing flames became watery blurs. What witchcraft kept those fires burning in the rain filled her with anxiety. On either side of the flames, between the fires and canvas lean-tos, caged bimembrae sat on haunches or lay in a fetal position. The great muscular, hairless beasts with horned heads were exactly how she envisioned them during the repeated gray-skin rituals. Disconcerting, yes, but the unfortunate part, the part that chilled her blood, was how she felt about the beasts. Not fear or trepidation nor awe but camaraderie. Grander than that.

Intimacy.

And fury.

Fury unlike any Indrasena ever experienced because the gray-skins had hunted and captured these majestic creations as any common animal, creatures proud and intelligent, heartfelt, complex that belonged in vast and wondrous mountains able to roam and breed and love; *live* instead of waiting to die at the hands of cowards, cowards who poked and prodded and jabbed spears, cowards unafraid protected by metal bars. The hopelessness infesting the bimembrae was the same that rotted her will while she wasted away in the pit, and what she ~~wanted~~ *needed* was to be free and punish the torturers, the abductors.

She had no realization of growling until the growl died and she collapsed to the table.

"Huh," uttered a throaty voice.

Indrasena arched her back and rolled her eyes up as far as they could go. "Who speaks?"

"Me old friend."

Wood and nails creaked as someone in the rear of the tent groaned, the groan an echo of Pater's father rising from a chair after a prolonged sit. More creaking between heavy steps. One foot landed harder than the other, also scraped. She whipped her head to the side. The tall fellow entering her eyesight was heavyset, not fat but robust in a powerful way. Gray salted his shoulder-length tresses and bushy beard. Familiarities—that bulbous nose and style of dress, the brown leather jerkin and pants stained green in places—did she know him?

She licked her lips with a tongue that had gone dry, then mumbled, "You are?"

"Praedator."

"Hunter? Named by profession?" She shook her head.

His smile was malformed, a product of the right cheek pulling back while the left stayed expressionless. On that side of his face a scar started at the corner of his mouth to cut through his beard over his jawbone as a river did a meadow before the scar faded into orangey hair. He pitched a crooked thumb towards the outside. "Saeva call me Praedator."

"Yet that is not your name."

He leaned over and stared. When she tried turning away, he grabbed her chin and yanked it in his direction, the force of his grip muting her shriek while the thumb and forefinger of his opposite hand parted her left eyelid. "Eyne. Yellower than afore. Where dots now be spots. Saevorum witchry. Wife right." He snickered. "Me not believe if not see."

Me in place of I and missing verbs. Plebes new to Calasade talked in such a manner, but this man was not—no, he had been in Calasade for decades and not cared enough to learn how to better communicate. His stance—head cocked, a shoulder dipping low—that face she pictured fuller and marked with fewer lines.

"*You?* Pater's venator bestia from when, when—you, *Hunter-Man?*"

His snicker graduated to laughter as he vanished from sight. Upon returning, he set a bucket on the table. "Ceno corde."

She despised herself, behaving the petulant child in biting her lip and shaking her head at the order to eat the heart. Was this the best rebellion she could summon?

Pitiful, *sickening.*

Anger boiled within and built, kept building until she thought it might erupt through her hands she was helpless to keep from reclosing and reopening. Heat collected in her palms, heat that got hotter and hotter. Instead of escaping, the energy coursed into her chest, throat where it seemed to swirl and congregate before something—an emotion, thought, intent?—wraithlike swept into and shot from her mind's eye.

An amber orb.

The orb hurtled outside the tent, hung and spun in the air, whizzing, then exploded into shards of light careering into the cages.

In unison, bimembrae roared.

How, what, what had just happened? Had the orb been real?

Pater's hunter bent over, guffawing while slapping his knee. "Me right! Grubs eats heart, you eats grubs. Not enow grubs to make beasts attack but feel you they do. To cast stronger magic might take long time. You babe, so..." He picked up and shook the bucket. The heart wet and heavy slopped inside. "Ceno corde. *Now*. Days coming you train. For weeks. Mayhap months. Years. Whichever. Me wants chrysae. Wife demand ship to sail way. Be free of war you help Saeva start."

She was unsure what any of those things meant beyond eating bimembrorum hearts and controlling the beasts. In response to that, she gasped, "Nulla." Over and over even as Pater's hunter whistled and waved to a gray-skin outside.

The gray-skin gave a single nod then disappeared from the tent's opening. She was still whispering nulla when the gray-skin came back. In his arms lay a bundled mess of a young man dirtier and bloodier than she. Indrasena had not seen him since the day their familia fell into servitude and were parted to satisfy a handful of debtors.

Her brother.

"You eat or frater die," said Hunter-Man as if discussing the weather. "Train or he die. Fail lesson, he get hurt. *You* get hurt. Me put grubs in you fun places. His. Give no medicine this time. Refuse, me cut off toe, finger, tit, nose. Make ugly you. Ugly him.

Give…" He traced his scar. "We take frater cock, berries. Feet and hand. Tong—"

She punched the table, screamed, *"Please…stop…this!"*

Praedator continued in that lifeless way of speaking. "We near kill frater afore in other pit. He no power. Pater used up. Teacher though. What success demand we do. Me life in balance. Wife life in balance. You threaten, be stupid when magic come, frater die. Pater die. Mater die. Want see parens?"

She nodded and wept.

He motioned to another gray-skin lurking behind the one carrying her brother. "Dungen. Fortrist." The hunter turned back to her. "Me say true. Do what told, we care for you, familia. Each live. Believe me words, girl?"

Indrasena blubbered. Again, she nodded.

XVII

SCRUTARI

"Dominus," Caderyn almost yelled at the threshold of the tablinum. Custom dictated he wait for the proconsul's signal before entering the room intended for official business, but he ignored tradition since an agitated adversary was an adversary less prone to stratagem and more susceptible to revealing things they wished hidden. "How do you fare this morn, Lepidus?"

"Same as any other." The proconsul was gruff in voice and how he spun around to glare across the desk, his shoes scraping the floor. "I stand irritated over the tardy arrival of clients. Have you come to say you are off yet again for remnants of a camp you will never find?"

A smile cloaked Caderyn's frustration and aches from two days of searching, his exhaustion from the hiking and awakening-riddled nights. While Jana had not repeated her nighttime lingering, his tossing and turning—worrying over when she reappeared, whether next time she slipped into bed beside him—had frayed his nerves. "I came to inform you our search nears completion. We divided the woods into sections. Today we finish the third and start on the last."

"Wonderful. Be sure to report naught at day's end."

Caderyn sat on the daybed minus an invitation, took satisfaction in Lepidus's lips squishing into a thin, disapproving line. Agitation had beset the proconsul; that was plain. "Has the artist finished his recreations of Indrasena's muralis?"

"Sloths besiege me. By the morrow or I will skin him." The proconsul sighed, shuffled pieces of parchment he whisked off a stack, and—without looking up—uttered, "I assume you have a request. Lend voice to it and see it denied."

"A letter of introduction."

"For what purpose?"

"So I can meet with the commander of Floridus's watchmen."

Lepidus looked up, brow furrowing to push the row of skin over his nose into a point. "The praefectus vigilum? Why?"

"I thought it evident."

"It is *not*." He retrieved a cherry from a bowl sitting at the desk's outer edge and rolled it between his thumb and forefinger.

Caderyn sat, tapping his knee, he the teacher gawking at a student who had failed to grasp the easiest of lessons. The irritation overcoming the proconsul made itself obvious in how the proconsul went from his typical pale hue to that of the fruit he juggled.

"I am *waiting*. Why do you wish to meet the praefectus vigilum?"

"Someone in a vigilis position may have information regarding sects."

The joints of Lepidus's jaw bulged in the moment of silence that passed. Through clenched teeth, he hissed, "What *kind* of sects?"

A chuckle had reached Caderyn's throat before he gulped—sheer deliciousness needling Lepidus. "Ones that help servae flee."

"You think she *escaped*?" Lepidus missed catching the cherry.

It dropped and rolled, hit Caderyn's boot. He picked it up and placed it on the pedestal. "Some of your custodes might be associated."

"You cannot be serious. You believe those I employ *sympathetic* to servae?"

"How without help does someone cart her off your estate with that road being the single avenue out?"

"By going over the crags—"

"Sounds easy, huh?" Caderyn loosed a fit of sardonic laughs. "No meadows populate these mountains. To hike in them is to circumvent trees and boulders and fight through heavy thickets, stumble over unseen roots and rocks, trudge across swampy ground in places, rough terrain in others, go around lakes, and scale cliffs or walk for hours if not days locating a safer path. Sprained ankles come easy. So does breaking a leg or falling to one's death. This without watching over an unwilling traveler struggling to free herself every step of the way. All-the-while, at any moment, the penchant for attacks exists. Bears, wolves, lions, snakes; the gods know what else. If Indrasena draw breaths, Lepidus, you can wager your entire fortune someone you trust aided her."

Lepidus groped for another piece of fruit from the bowl, muttering as if he were alone. "But why would she leave when I promised her" —he cleared his throat, spoke up—"Did you say *if* she was alive?"

"Cease acting the—mayhap this is no act. Mayhap you are stupid, blind, and naïve."

"Do *not* speak to me in such manner!"

"I will talk whatever way sparks your emotion to obtain the answers I need." Caderyn went quiet for a few moments to let his disobedience gain weight and sink in. "Aio, *proconsul*, I believe *your* custodes or servae involved if Indrasena—Let me be frank. I investigate these woods not for an old campsite but for a corpse."

The proconsul gulped. "For anyone to kill a creature that exquisite—"

"Her beauty may be the cause if a custos or servus made advances she rebuked and they killed her out of shame or fury."

"*None* would dare!"

"Oh? Is your control over others absolute? These are the potentialities, harsh as they are. Two of them indicate you house an infidel. We cannot ignore any possibilities regardless the discomfort they cause."

"An itch or crick in the neck is a discomfort. What you discuss—"

"Is *again* a possibility. Supply me a letter of introduction. Papyrus. House seal."

The proconsul hung his head. "Aio."

"About Jana. Earlier you said you wanted the...?" Caderyn trailed off, trying to lead Lepidus into divulging Jana's official title, but the proconsul set his jaw and protruded his chin. "You said she was to accompany me to Floridus, yet I have not seen her as of late and I wish to leave as soon as the search ends."

"She went to fetch herbs for treating a servus fallen ill. Whether she will be back to go with you..." He shrugged. "I can tell you the location and name of the inn where she rents a room when in-town."

Auspicious news abounded. His employer humbled, Jana's absence prolonged. The high Caderyn got compared to the elation of playing Imperatori. Two things could have sweetened the moment: a strong belt of brew and learning what capacity Jana filled. She had declared in Polus she was once a slave to Lepidus. Able to go elsewhere, why did she stay?

"The inn's location and name then," Caderyn agreed. A ruse, for he had no intention of soliciting Jana's aid. "And the letter of introduction. It is imperative I meet the vigilum."

"I insist," Lepidus mumbled, "that you conceal the truth of why you look for Indrasena. Whether she fled or someone took her, either circumstance shows weaknesses I cannot afford exposed."

"What shall I say if hounded?"

"That you are her cousin is convincing since you are both educated and your accents are similar. As are you, my ancilla is a former nobilis from Fors albeit much farther north."

Information of Indrasena freely given was a sign to press. Though not with impatience. Caderyn bent and grabbed the cherry from the pedestal, then took his time consuming it. Shock value never hurt. "How did you come across Indrasena?"

The bridge of Lepidus's nose had wrinkled, upper lip furled. "Her familia owed a substantial amount for grain to an associate of mine. He needed money more than servae. Me being in the opposite position, I purchased enough of the debt to claim the girl. Her cousin would know of their destitution because of her brother's..." Lepidus squinted.

"Aio?"

"Unimportant."

"What is it? Anything, the slightest detail, can be instrumental."

Lepidus looked off to the side.

Caderyn rose to leave because whatever the proconsul might say constituted a lie. "As you wish. I leave you to prepare for your clients."

He passed from the tablinum into the atrium to the desperate sound of Lepidus yelling after him. "Indrasena's cognomen prior to joining my house was Vivianus. Use Nicon as your forename. The praefectus vigilum—Atilius—is prejudiced against those of foreign ancestry."

Nicon Vivianus. The name imparted haughtiness.

Two frustrating days later Caderyn bordered on quitting the woods. Scratches covered his hands and forearms—cheeks, too, if the stinging were any indication—and sweat running into his eyes made finding signs difficult. To do something so simple as breathe was arduous. The afternoon had grown unseasonably hot mid-day and the thin mountainous air thick, muggy. His right leg further hampered his progress. Each hesitant step shot twinges into his hip and spine after he had climbed atop a pile of brush to get a better view and the brush had caved and caused his knee to twist.

That had been hours ago far northwest.

He now headed back to the villa, fatigued and feeling beaten, tramping in the fourth section as barren of signs as the three before it. At least Indrasena being alive was plausible and he had owned the foresight to prepare for such an eventuality. With the artist finished recreating smaller representations of Indrasena's mural he was ready to question people in Floridus. The bad news was Jana's return and her insistence upon joining them. She brought further discontent to his mental well-being by lurking too close whenever they occupied the same space, by tempting him with her smell and seemingly unintentional brushes. She had the tendency to dawdle while saying goodnight when seeing him to his cubiculum on those occasions Lepidus retired early. Her innuendos and Caderyn's bits of memory nicking like jagged shards of glass were convincing arguments he and she had slept together aboard the ship.

This had put Caderyn on the verge of throwing up his hands and roaring in vexation, of frequenting a tabernum and drinking until he forgot his nightmare of Elianna and the cave, her death. Her request.

Become the man I love.

The quiet before the storm was ending too soon.

Consumed as he was with his thoughts, his trespass into a small clearing never registered, and he failed to spot what tripped him face-first into a beck. The brook's pebbles dug into the heels of his hands as he did a push-up to rise and streams of water ran off.

Done. Past time to concede the hypothesis Indrasena's murder was a worthless idea. Maybe surrender on the whole matter. Go home. Slip into oblivion.

Back on his feet, he raised both hands, stretching to get rid of the stiffness in his shoulders while scanning the northern rim that overlooked the clearing. The woods in this area were miles deeper than the impression they gave from the vantage point of Lepidus's villa. Trees—tall as they were—had hidden the plateau of no concern if not for the beck's source; a waterfall, the cascade too great to result from just melting snow.

A fine campsite up there, should a lake for water and food be present.

Caderyn rush-limped, alternating between checking for obstacles to glaring straight ahead, cursing his stupidity and blindness and puzzling over how to scale the rim lame. Closer to the plateau he grinned with relief. The rim's cliff slanted and its rocky outcroppings eased the way by creating a staircase of sorts. At the top he caught his breath and gawped at a pristine mountain lake fed by snowmelt on all sides except for the northern end where a river ran off another cliff, its waterfall louder than the one that brought him here.

Three-fourths around the lake came a break in the woods. Among the tree-stumps were planks erected into X's over ground carpeted in wood-shavings and bark. Beyond the tree-stumps he discovered a cave. Inside was a pan and pot, a cooking grate covering a shallow fire-pit. Shoeprints were indiscernible due to the cave's dimness, but back outside, once he studied the grass, he inspected deep impressions alongside shallow ones. Next to the lake he found a third set of prints, these made by slenderer feet. A woman? It appeared she was dragged where the footprints became lines in the claylike mud of the shore with larger tracks in front and to either side, deepest at the heels.

Irregular, too.

The right mark dug in farther than the left at the inner part of the foot, symptomatic of a person with a busted or unhealed—

Caderyn straightened.

The pincernus fetched a mug from a shelf. "You are at the wrong place for avoiding past demons."

"Yet I am to meet one. A tall fiend carrying a broad-axe. He has a bulbous nose, messy beard, carrot-colored hair past his shoulders. Also limps."

"You describe the hunter of beasts."

"Acteon is present?"

"Of a sort. Are you Caderyn Fortis?"

He nodded.

The pincernus gestured at a bald man in a beige toga who sat at a table and was busy setting up Imperatori. "Proconsul Lepidus—"

Lepidus...

"Acteon sends his regards and fulfills his debt through me."

Unnecessary, going to where the river began for Caderyn to see it capable of supporting a boat or raft and that its grade was slight, rapids mild beyond the waterfall. He went anyway on the hope of disproving his suspicion, that he now hunted a friend of over ten years, a man familiar with Lepidus and the proconsul's villa, able to camp in wilderness and await the chance to steal a woman worth a fortune, a man clever enough to devise an escape and strong enough to carry or force his victim miles over rough terrain. Such a man who had taken contracts from nobles to hunt exotic beasts would have known if a magum bestia were in unrepayable debt.

Caderyn eyeballed the river coursing through the ravine, wondering whether the river dumped into Mali Sea or delivered Floridus fresh water. Questioning townspeople was useless if the river dumped into the sea and Indrasena's captors hauled her aboard a ship bound for unknown ports.

He checked the downing sun and decided he was too short of daylight for returning to the villa, much less exploring a river that stretched for who know how long even were his leg a nonfactor. As true, if he stayed, the hours counted too few for fashioning a spear and fishing and he needed to eat—maybe try getting back to the villa, but then again, hunger was less worrisome than Jana standing at his bedside.

That decided it. He hunted for a rock with an edge, another flat but still rough and decent for sanding, then a third with a point. With the tender and stick he collected they provided the tools for creating a fire in the cave. The stick he used as a spindle and placed it inside the notch he had drilled into the wood sanded flat. He was out of practice since his military days and neglected to apply enough pressure, but as the sun winked its last light and his arms were tiring, the tender lit. The subsequent fire he fanned into life illuminated how the campers entertained themselves.

Bones from an unidentifiable animal made into dice for playing Numeri, a rectangular board marked off in grooved squares. Imperatori. That was surprising. Acteon had disliked the game when he and Caderyn were friends, claiming the play was too slow and required too much concentration.

The question of to whom Acteon sold Indrasena left Caderyn grasping. He could have better guessed had the beast-hunter visited more often after wedding a woman Caderyn never met. He had seen the beast-hunter, what, on a handful of occasions in the past three or four years to gamble and drink. Those occasions stopped once Caderyn quit his addictions. Months upon months came and went without a word, then that messenger had shown up, saying that Acteon waited at the Twisted Vine to settle an ancient debt.

Caderyn laid prone to settle in for the night. His last thought before drifting into a deep sleep even with the pangs in his belly, leg, and back and the lack of a blanket for padding concerned Lepidus. Had the proconsul paid two thousand chrysae due to the hope it convinced Caderyn to fight on the Bleeding Grounds or because the proconsul held Acteon dear-to-heart?

In the morning, after awakening and stretching his limbs outside the cave, Caderyn listened to birds chirping and admired the waves rippling across the lake, the water numbing his palm as he cupped a few sips. Chilly—a gust of wind making him shiver—he rubbed his arms and urged himself to get moving, but common sense stayed him, argued this was to be his last foreseeable peace and he ought to take advantage. From here forth, should his suspicions of Acteon prove correct, things turned ugly.

Here forth started with his leaving this oasis.

So he loitered. First by raising his foot and rotating it, working soreness out of his ankle, then massaging his knee, studying the ground. Pebbles littering the lake's shore showed every color. Pyrite so similar to the gold for which fools took it sparkled in the morning sun. The ridges of smoky white mica shone like crystals. Milky quartz. Brown granite. He sat for a spell under a pine—its fallen needles a nice cushion for his natis—and watched trout jumping for flies. An occasional duck flew in.

Around mid-morning he departed and whistled even as the cliff jarred his leg and spine. The clearing entrapped him in crosswinds that penetrated his clothing and made his earlier chill seem summery. Nevertheless his whistling continued. The beck's babbling was an excellent accompaniment, put a spring in his not so rhythmic steps as the brook slowed in flatter terrain and quickened when the width of the stream lessened and the bed descended. Currents played a magic trick.

Here are stones.

There they are not.

For minutes he leaned against a pine's rough exterior or the silken texture of aspens, enjoyed a moment in which he and a black squirrel sitting on a branch participated in a stare-down contest. Precious seconds lent opportunities to watch spotted chipmunks dart from their dens in spite of their craven spirits.

Not everything he considered paradise-sent. Gnats pestered. Mosquitos stung. Why they buzzed in this season was mystifying. Perhaps they hung on until snow-weather approached.

Snow...

How picturesque these mountains blanketed in white.

Nigh dusk he left the woods and walked onto Lepidus's grounds. In rounding the villa, he and Jacob collided. It was as if nothing had hit the big man whereas Caderyn found himself on the ground, pain in his lower back emanating thanks to how hard his ass had landed.

Jacob beamed. "Ah, our Caderyn. A bit worse for—"

Caderyn grumbled and stood, leaned to the side and watched as Mathis, Lepidus, and Jana rounded the same corner that Jacob had. Jana at the rear soon caught up with and passed the two men.

Was it anger or exertion that colored her cheeks so rosy?

"Asinus," she seethed. "Do you know what could happen in these...your absence worried me *sick*. I have already lost someone I...Why are you so late in returning?"

"I hurt my leg," Caderyn replied, feeling a little boy tardy for dinner. "So I stayed in the woods." His gaze alit on Lepidus red-faced and crossing his arms. "The river north. Where does it lead?"

"To Floridus's aqueduct. Why?"

"Who told you of the debts that Indrasena's familia owed?"

Jana jabbed Caderyn's chest. "No apology? Or explanations? Instead you ask about that cunnus? You..." She slapped him and stomped off, vanishing around the corner.

Rubbing his cheek, Caderyn looked back to Lepidus. "Who alerted you to Indrasena's familia?"

The proconsul scoffed. "I fail to comprehend—"

"Instrumental, remember?" Disgusted, Caderyn shook his head. "Any detail can be vital. The debts, Lepidus. Who told you?"

The proconsul glared downward, seconds later at the sky, then off in the distance.

Caderyn squeezed his hands into tight fists and limped two strides. "Lepidus, I am sick of your secrecy."

The lone retort from the proconsul was the grinding of teeth.

"I *said*—"

"I heard you!"

"Who told you of Indrasena?"

"Acteon. What of it?"

"You petulant, miserable..." Caderyn wiped his lips. "Do you hold the beast-hunter so dear you opt for protecting our best suspect?"

"I prefer to discuss the relationship you and *my* Jana share."

My ancilla. *My* Jana. Everything and everyone to him was a possession. Caderyn's fingernails dug into his palms. "Why protect Acteon? You must have suspected him."

The proconsul huffed through his nose. "Acteon is my familiare. He has been since saving me from a bear in these woods. If you are proposing he betrayed me—"

"I am *stating* it. When did you last see the beast-hunter prior to Indrasena's disappearance?"

Lepidus stuck out his chin.

"You will not say?"

"Nulla."

Caderyn took another step forward and cocked his fist. The hand that grabbed his wrist was crushing. He wrestled his arm free and spun to face Jacob. "Why stop me?"

"Your clouting him will not get him to say what you wish to hear."

He raised his palms in mock surrender. "You, Mathis, and I are going to Floridus at daybreak. Besides asking if anyone saw Indrasena, we will inquire about the beast-hunter. Have Jana scribe a list of nearby stabula and hospitia and their locations on wax tablets. I thought to approach her, but...well, you saw how mad she was."

Jacob scowled. "Verum? Acteon a plagiarius?"

"Aio." Caderyn described the evidence, making sure Lepidus heard every syllable. He went inside to eat and bathe, rest for tomorrow.

In hindsight he should have prepared for the night.

XVIII

MEDICA

Caderyn requested the cook deliver his dinner to Indrasena's cubiculum and left the servus coquula more bone than meat, her outward condition poor not just in being underfed but bearing the scars of abuse. More and more his opinion of the proconsul withered. The world, as well, and divinity—how perverse the gods for allowing slavery, murder, rape, war. Sad people capable of bringing change preferred the status quo. And ironic those who rose from the dregs bent on making a difference ultimately mirrored the snobs they despised and forgot what it was to be destitute absent hope, fed by starvation.

Worse than any of the aforementioned were his kind, the lamenters who could have effected change but never considered doing so until after joining the futile downtrodden. Their steps got heavier, decrepit, like his did now as he limped across the peristylium to the bath-chamber and lumbered up the small staircase, taking care with his throbbing knee and ankle. Jana being a healer could help—he touched the cheek she had struck—no, not an intelligent idea soliciting her treatment.

Inside the chamber he paused, confused why his soles were warming and a cloud of steam hovered over the sunken bath before remembering the staircase, and realizing the balnei floor was higher than those of other first-level rooms, this extra height providing space for the bath's hypocaust.

No, nary a body to go dirty nor toe vulnerable to the coolness marble otherwise imparted.

Caderyn shook his head at the injustice of Lepidus basking in comfort while servae slept in the open, undressed, and slipped into the water, sitting on a ledge that submerged him up to his chest. He trained his gaze on shelving holding towels and robes. On the lowest shelf was...fatty-hued bars.

Soap.

Of course. Olive oil was unbefitting of a proconsul, what with the leftover residue.

Twice had Caderyn been fortunate enough to come across soap in a communal bath reserved for the highest of nobilia and here Lepidus stacked bars of it on a shelf. What else to expect of a balneum displaying ornate mosaics of nymphs locked in sexual congress with a mortal man bald and representative of the proconsul.

Having seen enough, Caderyn closed his eyes. Images came. The lake, the black squirrel, pines and aspens, crystal-clear mountain streams that widened and deepened into the ocean. Jana. Always Jana. The thought of her evoked what he best recalled of her from the ship, fieriness and antipathy over conditions of the crew, the man infirmed. Numerous the times she treated the dying fellow and blasphemed the gods for scourges or cursed the retched captain. Once, at twilight, she and Caderyn had been standing at the bow, she withdrawn and sad looking out over Mali Sea.

Tears streamed her cheeks as she bemoaned, "He will die. Naught I can do." And gripped the railing so hard, the knuckles of her petite hands colored white. "Morbus gallicus does not appear at the snapping of fingers and commence to delirium. There are *detectable* signs. Fevers, blotches, sores. These got ignored. Why?"

Unable to resist holding her, he wanted her because she was beautiful, yes—sensual, yes—but beyond that, profounder, he yearned due to her compassion.

Now, as then, he fantasized her kiss, but unlike the night on deck, envisioned her breasts small and firm, nipples erect, chest coloring, the rise and fall of her stomach under his caress, her mound covered in wheat-colored pubis. He massaged his cock, imagined her sex encompassing his while she clawed at his shoulder blades and their gazes locked.

The eyes peering back were apple-green instead of jade.

Elianna.

He waited to go flaccid, for the overwhelming guilt to dissipate. Craved for solitude. Ached to be isolated from temptation. Had he been on the lake's shores basking just this morning?

Caderyn splashed the water and got out, reached across the tub and grabbed a toga off the shelf. Thick yet rested light on his shoulders. Soft. Luxurious. Nothing save the finest.

Barefoot and dressed, dirty clothes and filthy boots in hand, he exited the balneum and walked across the peristylium, was halfway through the tablinum when Lepidus stomped out the atrium and vanished along the hall leading to the villa's exit.

"Good riddance," Caderyn mumbled, and entered Indrasena's cubiculum, tossing the soiled clothes on the wardrobe's floor before laying on the bed. He laced his fingers and put his hands behind his head, stared at the robins. His musings went from the birds to the Thermopolium de Calasade and meeting Jana. He pictured her branded forearm, the way the sun shone on her blonde hair, how her apple-green...

Jade. Not apple-green.

Elianna begged, "Let not another tempt you." during his dream of the cave, but what if...?

"During the daytime Jana was a constant at your side following a night you spent together in the cabin at the stern. Whether you could have done anything drunk as you were..."

What if Jacob had elaborated? Would I, Caderyn wondered, have gone to Floridus and gotten drunk or now embrace an exquisite woman?

Had he already?

The ship, the damn ship. The damn drink.

He concentrated, pushed at recalling more than hedonistic flashes of memory, naked skin, parted lips, moans of pleasure, climatic shudders. Here, laying in this bed with fists-clinching-discomfort in his groin and an unbearable urgency to be fondled, did his longing's intensity mean the recollections were figments of his imagination, that there had been no release for these caged-up desires?

Thoughts turned in on themselves. Pressure built, as always, until there came a crux when the manner of relief did not matter and he settled for—

—he wiped his lips.

The storm was definite regardless whether he remained lonesome or went after his desire. Thoughts turning, churning melded into the darkness of his mind's eye where quiet reigned. Peace. Solitude. The lake. Birds chirping. Elianna dying, gasping.

Become the man I love.

Blackness again. Serenity. Again. He dreamt of floating on the lake.

"Caderyn."

The sound of his name came from the firmament. Who called a second time? Familiar the woman's voice drawing, pulling, beckoning.

"Caderyn!"

He jolted awake, forehead butting against...what, who? Blonde hair whipped amid pained cursing and Jana shaking her head as if to rid her vision of stars.

"I suppose," she said, "I deserved that after slapping you."

He rubbed the soreness below his hairline. "Why are you here?"

"To treat you." She held up strips of bandages in one hand, a small jar with the other. "For your cuts and ankle and knee."

Caderyn sniffed. "*Whoof.* What is in the seriola?"

"Saliunca conferva. Never mind the flatulent aroma. This ointment will hasten your healing and defend against festering." She eyed him toe-to-head. "Unfortunate no balm can cure the rot inside."

"What is that supposed to mean?"

"You are drenched. I wonder whether your sweating owes itself to drink, the lack thereof, or the wife who haunts you from beyond the grave."

"You are yet cross."

"A bit." One half of Jana's mouth curved upward. "You are quite naked." She arched an eyebrow. "Such display I have not seen since aboard ship."

His asking should have been easy, but something unseen and unforgiving gripped his gut. "Did we...?"

"What, fututio?"

He nodded.

She looked off to the side. "I wish to apologize for striking you. The night of your absence, I worried. Was he attacked by an animal, did he fall off a cliff, is he out there injured, dying? I pestered myself with these things over and over. For you to show up looking...happy? Nulla. *Peaceful.*" She took a deep breath. "As for your question..." The blush that overcame her colored scarlet. "I wanted you from the beginning. Some of the reasons are apparent whereas others I cannot comprehend...Must we discuss this?"

"I need to know what happened, if I should..." Feel guilty was the wrong thing to say. No doubt those words would upset her and ruin any chance he had of learning what had transpired. "Go on. Eleison."

Her cheeks swelled with the air she blew. "Cannot comprehend why I wanted you. You are far from handsome and very broken. That was evident when you stepped inside the Twisted Vine. Yet I ~~am~~ *was* drawn in a way I have never been to anyone." She gulped. "Your...*ugh*, why is this so difficult? I am hardly inexperienced at my age and still, with every word spoken I am..." She pointed at her stomach.

"Fluttery," he said, nodding in case his murmur was too quiet.

"Aio, altum." She tapped her foot, the attempt of getting nerves under control obvious in her eyes squinting and lips pressing together. "Your rejecting me at Thermopolium de Calasade should have ended my fixation, but I thought...made up the excuse you refused due to your wife. I assumed she lived despite hearing words that hinted otherwise. Not until we rode for Dahak did I learn the details of Elianna's murder."

Jana's stare bordered on a glare. What did she want him to say? He opened his mouth. Closed it.

"Jacob told me," she explained, her jaw clenched. "I believed I could get over you, hearing she was dead and that you, you declined me because you did not want me. Am I so unattractive?"

"You are...you are...beau—" The word got stuck.

"You find me pretty?"

He nodded.

"Your saying so could have saved me considerable fret. On the ride to Dahak I wondered why you shunned me when I was not despising you for drinking. Then, upon boarding the ship, from out of nowhere your behavior changed. You acted kind only to me. The attention made me feel special. Each day and night, such tight quarters, the situation. We talked. About everything. The dearer our friendship grew, the greater I hankered for you. Your drunkenness, my taking advantage mattered no longer. Aio, I was that desperate because my coveting you was that extreme.

"We were this close" —she raised her thumb and forefinger a hair-width apart— "to having suh, suh, sex in the deckhouse. Getting you ready took a *long* time. Was a *lot* of work. But you...got almost inside me. I felt your...*you*. You pulled away, talked of Elianna and her murder, how you think yourself responsible. So much outpouring of emotion not for me."

"I...Apologies."

"For loving Elianna even to-day? *Asinus*. Your devotion is what every wife beseeches the gods for when her own husband proves less than—" She protruded her chin, shaking her head and rolling her eyes, blinking. "You got up and left me laying there stunned and heartbroken, but your spurning managed one thing. Brought me freedom from my...I hated you. At least a little. Until the night on deck anyway. No friendly embrace how you held me. But again" —she laughed bitterly— "you hoodwinked me into thinking there was an us. Stupid. I should have anticipated your slights to come."

"What slights?"

She crossed her arms. "How can you be this obtuse?" Another shake of her head was followed by flared nostrils. "When we arrived home and you had recovered from the captain's bludgeoning, you behaved as if—you looked at me with a grieved expression and withdrew whenever I neared, even fled my presence on those few occasions we were alone. No reason given why. No explanation. *Naught* for me. Then to have witnessed you admiring Indrasena's mural, to have heard *her* name pass your—"

"Jana—"

"Hush. Speak no more." She approached the bed.

He feared she intended to lay beside him. Would he push her away or succumb to his urge of taking her?

"Sit up and turn," she told him. "After I apply saliunca conferva to your cuts, I will wrap your knee and ankle. Be on my way. Until I go let us have silence. I think" —her bottom lip quivered— "that is best, aio, notwithstanding Lepidus's departure."

"Where did he—?"

"Silentium." She rapped him on the crown of his head. "I said turn."

His reaction to her kneeling at his feet was surprising; a dark and foul-tasting swill born of her genuflecting as slaves did for their masters. She was no servant, this proud woman reduced to tears, and should not have been healing him, not after everything he had made her suffer. Caderyn reached for her, wanted to say go or maybe stay. What did which matter as long as her servicing him ceased?

"Do not." Her words softer than a whisper barely penetrated his ears.

His throat was tight, dry. "Jana..."

The glistening in her irises pleaded for mercy better than her mumbled beg of, "Eleison."

"All right." Caderyn focused on the balm's smell because that sulfur-stink was less offensive than savoring how she touched him, how her delicate fingers moved to his knee and lingered before sliding to his inner thigh. He tried not to flinch or enjoy the tingling sensations she spawned, tried to ignore the desire to pull Jana's hands farther up to where his real ache throbbed. In the end what he did was brace the back of her neck.

Qualm rifled her tone. "What? Why now?" But even while asking, she moved with his pulling and looked up, her lips parted.

"Sober," he said, hoarse, "I know what it is I do. I know what it is I want. And who." He leaned forward until his forehead rested on hers. "I want *you*."

"Caderyn..."

Was that her starting to pout or smile? Whichever, his kiss interrupted the expression. The kiss was gentle, shy, the tips of their tongues went forward then retreated, as if he and she took a collective moment in deciding whether they wanted to take this leap.

Then their mouths melded. Tongues again glanced and stayed to play. Her hand gliding up his thighs gripped his cock. The grip tightening as she went up was hardest when she ran her thumb over the tip and loosened when going downward. He removed her stola not with care but by ripping it. When he laid back, she straddled him, guided him inside her wet warmth. Caderyn glimpsed the Afterlife in how she moved her hips back and forth in slow and delicious half-circles. With ever increasing speed she whisked them farther and farther until he erupted in pleasure and she collapsed, both laughing as giddy children might.

XIX

CONFESSUM

Though perspiration stuck to him after the night's pleasures and his hours of sleep totaled few, Caderyn awoke reenergized and sporting an unusual grin. What did not greet him was Jana. The bed's width turned out to be too slender for the two of them, so late into the night she had slunk to her own cubiculum. Caderyn offered to join her, but she held to the opinion it was wiser if they avoided giving the servae reason to prattle. Jana had appended that were she to remain beside his naked body, they were apt to get far less rest than what traveling to and searching Floridus demanded.

Flutters in his stomach flapped into his chest and he could not say whether these wings of unrest were due to thoughts of Jana or nerves over the events of today which determined whether rescuing Indrasena met an abrupt end or began in fervency depending on the ability of Dock Operarius Judoc or Praefectus Vigilum Atilius pointing out a direction to follow.

Caderyn tapped his mouth while beseeching the deity Alea for good fortune and pictured her statue in Polus's marketplace, a marble effigy of the golden-haired goddess dressed in flowing blue robes and holding an offertory basket full of riches. The visualization strengthened his entreaty, helped settle his butterflies. Beneficial was sacrificing an animal; infinitely so were the sacrifice made at the statue's base, evidenced by the bloodstains on Alea's feet.

His prayer now ended, he sat up, groaning. His stomach muscles had not been this sore since his wedding night when

Elianna had pushed him beyond the brink of exhaustion. With a sigh, he pushed back the flood of memories, those familiar portends of depression. Would that he could for however long make his happiness stretch and be as the living embodiment of the painted robins.

Free.

Liberated from desperation and ill recollections of worse places and situations, the people who cast side-glances at him, their noses upturned. Worst was the pincernus in the Twisted Vine; to have sunk so deep that a *slave* mocked him. He had to leave that behind. Here was a new life, him being a stranger to everyone except Lepidus and Jana.

He hurried to get dressed and hesitated once the vest—the last of his attire—was in place. His gaze drifting to beneath the bed stopped on the spherical hilts of his swords. The mucrones had been needless since the swap at Ferrum Merx and he foresaw no cause for wearing weapons today, yet he bent over, making and unmaking fists, hands itching to grasp the iron.

"Our driver grumbles," said Jacob from the doorway, curtain rings jangling. "Meanwhile oxen stamp the ground and Mathis grouses. Old hag him. Jana, she complains of the heat. Tiny wonder she sweats, sitting inside the plaustrum since the proconsul appeared—you know those covered wagons have the single window. Irritated the proconsul, keeps shuffling those small paintings of the mural and staring at them as if he cannot decide which he prefers, and by now, with your standing and my blabbering, Jana suffocates." He waved come. "Let us go."

Caderyn straightened. The big man was armed. Odds were Mathis, too. Sager for Caderyn to leave his swords; an angst-ridden dock operarius was a laborer unforthcoming.

He slipped by Jacob, limp slight on his way to the atrium, and stopped at the impluvium. Again Caderyn took in Indrasena's steel-hued eyes and their amber dots, her beatific face, that partial smile, tousled mane. Whereas the view remained identical, the sensation viewing her instilled differed. Admiration had gone absent and in its place a desire burned to save the girl wherever she might be from whatever horrors she might have undergone and make her captors suffer, including his own friend. Maybe he owed his newfound determination to Jana's talented lovemaking or to intuition. His was always strongest days after sobering and his little voice whispered to him now that Indrasena was close, if not in proximity than investigation-wise. A fine day for answers this.

Encouraged, he headed past the lectus genialis and into the hallway, outside the villa, the temperature hot but not as boiling as the glower Lepidus gave while handing to Caderyn a copy of Indrasena's mural.

"Proconsul," Caderyn said, sticking the palm-sized painting inside his vest before facing the covered wagon. He blinked against the sunlight reflecting off bronze lion statues adorning the driver's seat; from the brightness, too, of the wagon's white canopied top. He passed along the side made up of planks varnished but unpainted. Leather suspensions that marginally stretched when he got in and walked to Jana perching on a bench screeched as Jacob mounted the steps and canted the wagon.

"Mayhap," quipped Mathis behind the big man, "they should have harnessed an oxen *herd* to the plaustrum. Or had you pull it."

Laughter hearty, Caderyn sat and reached for Jana. His timing was off. She raised the hand closest to him to scratch her shoulder and afterwards crossed her arms.

Jacob tipped his chin at her. "How many hours to Floridus?"

"Follow the lead of our tardy but sober and tireless exquisitor. Sit and get comfortable."

Lepidus had approached the wagon and stood between the double doors, offering an expression chiseled in stone. "Jana, you and *your* party are to lodge at Taurus Exsecti. Expect me at the inn come daybreak to discover what you learn."

He swung the doors shut with a clang.

A whip snapping and oxen grunting heralded the start of their journey made pleasanter for Caderyn by Jana's palm sliding against his, her skinny fingers interlacing his thicker ones. The softness of her skin brought on meditations of last night, the detail of his recollections enhanced through the regular squeaking of wheels that was hypnotizing.

Mathis dozed off several miles on. Jacob snored what turned out to be halfway.

Now in-private, Caderyn looked to Jana. "You said I was sober, that Jacob should do as 'our tardy but sober and tireless exquisitor'."

A slight smile played on her mouth as she traced his bottom lip with the pad of her forefinger. "You are those things and more."

"But my abstinence of drink will change, as it always does. You asked me in Polus what it is to battle my affliction." The sunlight coming in the wagon's single window fell slanted across her face and was a beautiful revelation of illumination and shadow. "Do you still wish to know?"

She nodded.

"To deal with drink is to experience an ever-repeating, unpredictable winter. Dry summers can last weeks, months— even a year or two—but sooner or later, pressure builds and I focus on the wrong things. *Dark* things. I turn inward. My moods are then periodic bouts of anger until those bouts swell into unwavering fury."

"Why do you tell me this? Is it to frighten me?"

"So you will recognize the signs."

"For what purpose?"

"So you may succeed where Elianna failed. I hope—*pray*—I have learned after her murder, that with support, a new location and fresh beginning, with some happiness..." He grunted, frustrated over losing what it was he wanted to say. Were all men this inept at conferring their weaknesses or was his inability to articulate a personal fault? "I tell you so you can save me from myself should...if you remain at my side."

Jana caressed his cheek. "The future is the Great Unknown. What is not a mystery? How I feel. Unafraid. I shall go nowhere."

"Judoc no work here," Barra said to Caderyn. The short and stocky, tan fellow Jana had interrupted loading barrels onto a cargo-barge scratched the side of his unshaven face, its flatness typical of southern islanders. His shaking, globular head mirrored that of Lepidus in that not a hair grew on it. "Judoc quit...mmm...couple moons ago. He—how you say?" Barra flicked his wrist and made a snapping sound. "He hard on workers. They not sorry see him leave. They say" —he jabbed a chopped-off thumb at himself— "me nice boss. Easy to be nice with higher pay. Not mind being from home now or cold or losing finger or working when head hurt from cervisae. A lot I drink. Easy to drink lots paid..."

Caderyn coughed, hiding his smile and tuning out Barra to subdue his burgeoning laughter. A good thing Mathis and Jacob had departed to check the hospitia and stabula else conversing with the new dock operarius last until sundown.

Jana scooted in between him and Barra. "Why did Judoc quit?"

The dock operarius leaned to the side and said to Caderyn, "He get money. Lotsa coin."

"See here." Jana poked the man's muscular, sweat-beaded chest. "I asked the question. You answer me."

"Woman. Water. Bad mix. Not tempt sea god. Me talk wild-man."

Wild-man? Caderyn frowned. He should have brushed his hair. Better he got it cut. He cupped Jana's shoulders and squeezed them through her leather jerkin, prompting her to move. Only after he nudged her did she take two miniscule steps, grumbling. Caderyn could no longer suppress his laughter. "From where did Judoc get his fortune?"

Barra stared with slits for eyes, mien slackening.

"Coin," Caderyn explained. "Where did Judoc get the coin?"

"Ah, me see. Hot this day. You. She. Drink cervisia at tabernum. Nice. Cool. Talk him give drink." Barra motioned at the line of buildings behind them that were at the top of a staircase and half surrounded the port. "Third place over."

"I should talk to the pincernus?"

Barra's gravel voice dropped to a conspiratorial level. "Big man keep eyne around. Ears in places listen."

"Big man?"

"Red hair. Limps."

Caderyn took an anxious step forward. "Was he called Acteon?"

"Me not know." Barra furrowed his thick eyebrows as his whisper further hushed. "Came afore Judoc quit, but me no forget. Scary big man. How you say man search for something he need and cannot find? Search-search-search here-there, corner-nook. Edgy! Mean. Crazy dog. He warn workers, 'Silentium or axe.' You go. Drink. Sit. Nice. Cool. Talk server. Judoc favorite place. Each eve, sometimes day, he—"

Despite her shorter legs, Jana was faster than Caderyn, leading their charge off the dock and up the weathered, sea-worn steps. Her lighter feet registered as the pitter-patter of children scampering whereas the stairs shimmied under his clunking. At the top, as she navigated the turn and was almost gone, he snatched her wrist.

Whatever the reason for her enthusiasm, Caderyn was glad for it. He had worried she might retard any success. "Judoc in the tabernum—on Alea's most charitable day she is not that generous. Let us assume Judoc is elsewhere. We will fare better should you go in without me."

Her nose scrunched. "I am unsure how things are in Fors, but here in Permia folk take a harsh view of women frequenting tabernae absent a chaperone."

"You went in alone at the Twisted Vine."

"That was in Polus where no one knew me and because I had no choice."

"Apologies for my asking, but Acteon is an intimidating man. The pincernus will be as tight-lipped as Barra and—"

"You are thinking honey is better temptation for the fly."

"Do not flirt more than necessary, eh?" He pulled her against him and smacked her butt harder than he intended. "You know, your smile and that dimple you get at the corner of your mouth makes kissing you irresistible."

"Could be the exquisitor has found a new affliction."

"Could be."

"Splendid to hear. What is my reason for seeking Judoc? Shall I play the jilted woman?"

"You are much too quick, Jana...?"

"My cognomen is Lepidus."

"Customary," he said, sheepish, "you adopted the proconsul's name upon joining his house. You know, we ought to change your affiliation."

"Oh?" She fluttered her eyelids. "Hints at betrothal do cause the wanton to swoon."

He chuckled. "So soon after last night and you are salacitas."

"I am *lascivious*." She kiss-pecked him. "But to-night after we finish investigating, you and me, we should talk."

'We should talk.' Those words shriveled his groin. "Has this to do with us?"

"Later, when there is plenty of time. Until then do not fret a truth of nuisance."

With that, she tramped the boardwalk, leaving his hands empty and him following as far as the window of the third building over where he leaned against the bannister to gaze out over the harbor. Sunlight glinted on the undulating sea that rocked anchored ships and moored boats, one of which Barra still worked, his occasional grunts audible during those moments din from within the tabernum did not drown out the dock operarius. Caderyn harrumphed. He expected the guffaws of drunkards and the clinking of mugs to entice him, but here, now—at least for now—temptation was nonexistent. How wonderful life to always be content, for—

The nappy hairs on the back of his neck rose.

Someone was watching him.

He play-itched his right shoulder and turned his head that direction, sighting nothing but trees. Seconds later he stretched, his arm hiding his peeking to the left. There—just visible around the corner of the farthest building—was a face too distant to recognize. He resumed watching the harbor.

Upon Jana's return and her putting a hand on his shoulder, Caderyn stared away from their onlooker and muttered, "Someone spies on us at boardwalk's end. Go back into the tabernum and circle round. We can trap whoever it is with my coming from this side."

Not missing a beat, speaking in a normal tone, she called him my sweet and explained their presence. "Mea dulcis, join me indoors and give your tired eyne a rest. The dock operarius can work unsupervised while loading the proconsul's wares."

Quick she was. "I prefer to stay here. Warm day, refreshing breeze. Lessens—" He gestured at his temple.

"I hoped your headaches gone." She sighed and patted her thigh, giving Caderyn the distinct impression she toyed with a decision. "Does your nose run as well?"

"Aio." He sniffled. "Is a brook."

"Mea dulcis," she said, her hesitancy perfect for lending the sense of authenticity, "let me wait alone for the proconsul and you take the opportunity for visiting the medicus. Describe your symptoms. Mayhap he knows a remedy."

"Remind me where his shop stands. I struggle to think."

"Walk beyond the boardwalk then to the street. The brown and green building."

He nodded as if the action hurt. "Appreciation."

She kissed him on the cheek and departed. Caderyn massaged his temples before ambling the boardwalk slow enough to give Jana the time necessary for passing through the tabernum. He kept his head tilted away from the sun, glad for his "headache" that nullified the difficult task of glancing around and pretending the spy continued to go unseen.

Twigs snapped upon his nearing the end of the boardwalk, a sign their spy was moving.

"Caderyn," Jana yelled.

He rushed around the building to find the spy scampering towards him. Quick as a rabbit the spy halted, spun, and bounded, shoving Jana to dash into the street. Caderyn gave chase, going around her as her rump hit the ground and her teeth clacked together. He pulled up limping thirty strides later.

Jana, red-faced, came up breathing as heavy as he. "Get a look at him?"

Caderyn shook his head. "You?"

"Nulla." She grinned the same half-smile that tempted him earlier. "Battered though my ego and natis are. The last you will massage to-night to make up for smacking it and causing that speculator to further bruise it."

"I have had worse orders. Did the pincernus—?"

"He was most helpful. Judoc lives nearby in a new domus four blocks outside the industrial area. Moreover, the pincernus confirmed Barra's information. Judoc came into rich coin, but refuses to say where or how."

"Well done." Caderyn wiped sweat from his forehead. "We should move with haste. Whoever that speculator was, he heads to warn Acteon."

"Tell me." Her hand slid into his and squeezed. "Has the brilliant exquisitor always been speedy at concluding the obvious?"

He laughed in spite of himself. "A bolt slicing across the astrum I am."

"Poor thing." Jana mock-pouted and turned him to her. She kissed him long, her mouth pressed up against his hard as her gentle fingers toyed with his hair.

After she pulled away, he guessed his own cheeks flushed like hers, but in him there was none of the sadness that clouded her irises. "What was the thing you wished to discuss?"

"Here?" She peered at the people around them. "I suppose we are anonymous enough lost among a crowd. We better be anyway, because what I did just now—Let us get moving. We can talk on the way."

They went ahead, but she said nothing as they routed between shoppers. Rather than dwell on the unsettling silence and why she was having trouble speaking, Caderyn focused on the hunger-inducing aroma of loaves baking, the buzzing of flies and ripening odors of fish, the brilliance of fresh greens and browning pies. From the shops of foodstuff he and she proceeded to burning metal and the banging of heavy hammers, the tinging of lighter ones. Now and again she or he pulled the other to circumvent gurgling and overflowing silanae where people filled water-buckets. Every stride taken with her staying quiet screwed his insides, but he refused to push her because he was reluctant to confirm his suspicions that whatever they shared was over.

We should talk.

When she spoke, the screwing of his insides worsened. He knew the end of their relationship was coming and he knew why it was coming. There had been signs unchecked until now; too late to keep from getting hurt.

"Talking," she admitted in a rush, "I anticipated it easy, yet we near the neighborhood of Judoc's house and still, I struggle with how to begin."

Contemplations had made him blind to the shinier walkways and deaf to the tranquil surroundings. They were not in the section where the rich lived in mansiones, but neither did they stroll the colluvio. Gone were the casulae with thatch roofs and flimsy walls, the cellulae that turned people into rats within small apartments. The domae here were middle-class, decent-sized, and hung onto a modicum of modesty.

"Neither of us," he said, going back to watching his feet, "at our age are without the tethers of past relationships...or" —his gut churned— "even current ones."

He mulled how Jana had declined his offer of joining her in her bed and how she had slunk away, contemplated her jealousy while speaking of Indrasena's mural and the proconsul.

"*...People would pay were the art's sheer lewd size advertised. Were her beauty. Or why he had the painting created. Let each customer admire its excruciating detail and marvel as I did and do and must and witnessed you doing the same.*"

Jana's concluding a client-meeting, such a role was for the domina, wife of the house. He pictured the lectus genialis inside Lepidus's atrium—the tiny bed symbolizing the sanctity of marriage—and reflected on what the proconsul seethed outside the villa on the morning Caderyn returned from the lake.

"*I prefer to discuss the relationship you and my Jana share.*"

How had he missed what those auguries revealed?

"You," Caderyn squeezed out his ever-constricting throat, "are married. To Lepidus. When you said you were unafraid and going nowhere, you meant you were staying with him."

Her stopping was so abrupt he took several paces before realizing he left her behind. Caderyn turned—had turning ever taken anyone so long?—and saw the color of her face go from pale to healthy to tomato-hued.

"Asinus," she hissed. "You assume I leave you."

"I cannot offer—" He had ran out of breath and his chest was too tight. He drew air harder to reap than it should have been and sighed so heavily his lips flapped. "Lepidus can give—"

"You..." She bit her bottom lip, shook her head then gave a glare capable of smelting iron. "You make the sound of a horse's mouth, but you closer resemble its other end. You..." The finger she pointed folded as Jana made a fist she slammed against her thigh. "I was servio to Lepidus."

"I have heard. Your dead husband's debts. You told me of those in Polus. Why not—?"

"Mention my marriage at Thermopolium de Calasade? Say during our negotiation I said if not for marrying Lepidus, I was to spend another decade cleaning his floors, licking his boots, eating scraps, getting beaten? Is a man who forced such an arrangement the type for whom you would work?" She again bit her bottom lip, but this time the biting did not dam her tears. "Lepidus has given the one thing of worth he could provide. My freedom. What I now want—nulla, what I *need*—is you."

Caderyn snorted. "Pretty words. Had I known—"

"You *were* aware. Aboard ship I explained the night we tried to fututio."

The drink. The damn drink. "You should have mentioned being married again last night." Had that been a few hours past? Frightening how such a short span of time seemed forever ago.

"Last night I was angry and sad and bewildered, especially when you kissed me. And I wanted you. How I *wanted you*. I did naught save what my heart demanded. It is this once, a singular chance, and I must take it. That is what I told myself because I dared not—after your acting hither-thither, the notion of us being an actual couple—I never dreamt of us lasting until you mentioned me saving you."

He hung his head. "I am a horse's natis."

Jana choked out a laugh. "Aio, and yet your newfound humility" —she came up to him, put her arms around his waist— "makes not kissing you unbearable."

He brought his lips to hers. "What are we to do?"

"That depends."

"On?"

"As you said, at our age, I am no girl and you are no boy. An emotion that comes in such a rush is infatuation. I think we both recognize this."

He nodded.

"But as I alluded inside the plaustrum, I am going nowhere *away from you*. Whatever is between us—whatever comes from it—is more than either of us have had for a long, long time. This is enough promise for me to throw the dice. What say you?"

"You ask me about gambling?" He shrugged, smiling. "It comes easiest when I have naught to lose and everything to gain."

"Naught? You wager sixty-five thousand chrysae."

"If we can find and save Indrasena. Acteon seems a simpleton, but he is anything other. The flawed bet is waging Judoc or the vigilum has an inkling where Acteon took her."

"Then what we shall do is settled. Should we get a lead on Indrasena, I will inform Lepidus of my desire for divortium after she is safe and he has paid you. The money is unimportant to me. Squalor, however, renders you a real mess."

"And if we discover the girl is lost?"

"Then in the morn I tell Lepidus of my affair and demand he dissolve our marriage."

"And to think I wondered why you were enthusiastic for finding Indrasena despite you hating her."

"Amazing your lightning-quick mind." She patted his backside. "Verum, I do not hate the girl. Quite the opposite in fact. My mentioning that townsfolk pay to view her mural, when I slapped you—aio, I was jealous, out of my mind with invidia after seeing how you looked at her painting."

Unable to lie why he had stared, Caderyn cleared his throat. "Will Lepidus grant you divortium?"

Her eyebrows arched. "Oh, I think so. Upon learning I shared your bed he will deem me insalubrious to touch and unworthy of sharing his name."

JUDOC

Caderyn's grin strained his cheeks. "Which home is Judoc's?"

Jana pointed at a two-storied, gray-marble domus between two others but nearer to the street, as if the home were an afterthought and crammed in where space permitted. The roof was highest at the center, sloping on its four sides. A lack of soot on the chimney, the vibrancy of the terracotta, and cleanliness of the second-floor's arched windows denoted the house's recent construction. The lone door was on that floor, accessible through a tunnel-staircase going from the street and letting out on the balcony. A locked, grated gate blocked entry to the staircase. No windows were on the lower level since the upper alone served as living quarters—modern measures bent towards safety.

Here he had taken the pains to hire a cleptus in Mathis and then sent the thief on a search with Jacob right when circumstances demanded the thief's talents. Why, Caderyn wondered, had he ever considered himself possessed with foresight?

"What now?" Jana asked.

"We wait and hope that Judoc comes home after dark, if he is indeed gone."

"And if not? If a light shines in yon window?"

"We fetch Mathis from the Taurus Exsecti and visit Judoc in the dead of night." Caderyn expected him to mirror his high-strung successor Barra; such a man kept his door shut to strangers after dark. Either way, Judoc gone or at home, Jana and he required somewhere to sit for hours without raising suspicions. Nigh was a fountain dedicated to Caeruleus. Beyond that was...unable to tell what lay farther along besides houses, he ventured into the street. Close to where the road curved three blocks away was a quartet of vacant stools lined up on the sidewalk in front of a counter to a snack-eatery. The distance to the cafum was too great for a decent vantage point, but it was the best spot they—

Jana stepped beside him. "Judoc comes."

Already, with his having no chance to think how to question the man. Caderyn grabbed Jana's wrist. "You were with Albertus. Do *not* deny it!"

Confusion clouded her eyes for the briefest of seconds. Then her mouth set into a thin line. She punched his chest and went around him; he guessed to have her back facing the man Caderyn assumed to be Judoc, him of uncombed black hair and an overall haggard appearance due to a baggy stola and his hunching from too many years loading and unloading barrels. His sandaled feet shuffled on the concrete.

"Asinus!" Jana seethed, quiet enough to avoid drawing undue attention but at a level Caderyn was sure Judoc heard. "How dare you accuse me." Ever the actress, she shoved him. "Where was I?" Shove. "Verum?" Shove. "Out, oh aio, *out*."

Another push moved Caderyn next to the tunnel-staircase. The former dock operarius was almost upon them.

She carried on in that same hostile, loud undertone. "Out working until the rooster crowed. That is what I was doing. Where were you while I worked at the tailor's shop? You spent another night passed out in our bed. We have debts. *Mountains* of them." A final push put him in the ideal position for intercepting Judoc. "Thanks to your wasting our coin on whores and—"

"Sodes," the haggard man interrupted, shuffling foot-to-foot. "Domus be mine."

Caderyn cried, "Judoc, my old friend!" and slung an arm around the fellow, then whispered, "Do not flinch or cry for help. This will end in pain if you do."

A woman carrying a bucket on the other side of the street gazed at them. Caderyn smiled wide and waved with his free hand. She raised hers, paused, and—in a timid shake—returned his greeting.

He muttered to Judoc, "Invite us into your domus for vina and talk of days gone by. Use a calm and clear voice."

Judoc fetched a key from his pouch. After two or three nervous jabs, he slid the key home and unlocked the gate. "Cuh, cuh, come. Drink. Talk old ta, times."

Pivotal junctures in one's life, he thought, those instants you forever remembered with the clarity of yesterday, were supposed to be momentous and not something small—a silver gate squeaking open, sun glinting off a top corner before the gate clanged against the staircase it guarded, but that moment would persist until his dying breath, the moment everything changed which ended with Caderyn nudging Judoc up the stairs and following right behind.

From atop the balcony he checked whether the woman strolled away—she did—and said to the former dock operarius, "I will not hurt you unless you give me no choice. Inside."

Single-file they entered Judoc's house, the furnishings few; chairs and a table, a daybed. Caderyn shoved Judoc towards the table and sat across from him, pulling the copy of Indrasena's mural from behind his vest to put it between them. His glare was unwavering. "Where is she?"

The knot of the man's gullet bobbed. "I not know."

"Judoc, you are a terrible liar. Time runs short. So does my patience."

"Buh—"

Caderyn ticked his eyes at Jana standing to the side. "Look at her."

Judoc did.

"You aware who she is?"

He nodded. "She come to dock with proconsul once, twice."

"Jana is his wife. Also my amasia. I tell you of my relationship with her because you need to realize I am being honest with you. I tell you this because I wish to avoid her seeing my uglier half. She will, however, the next time I ask where is Indrasena and you lie. Give me your hand."

"Why?"

"I will not request it again." He had begun to rise when Judoc slid his quivering hand outward atop Indrasena's painting. Caderyn gripped Judoc's bony wrist, tugged, and took hold of the man's forefinger. "Each time you state an untruth, I will break a finger. This will hurt. You will scream. That is fine. Your windows are shuttered, the walls and door thick. I doubt anyone will overhear, though if they do and come to your aid or raise an alarm, again, things will end badly. Understand?"

Judoc gulped, nodded.

"Where did Acteon take Indrasena?"

"I not—"

He yanked Judoc's finger backwards. There was a loud snap followed by the man shrieking as he tried jerking his hand free, but there was no getting away. Jana had covered her ears and turned. Good. This would be easier without her looking. In hindsight, he should have asked her to stay outside.

Judoc stopped shrieking and started blubbering. Spittle ran down his chin as he acted every bit a helpless toddler bewildered at why he had been lashed while comprehending the punishment to repeat.

Caderyn grabbed the man's middle finger.

More shrieking. Greater blubbering. Judoc's horrified expression matched the desperation in his voice. "I tell who pay me! *Eleison*. No hurt. I tell where he have girl taken."

"He?"

"Praedator. Orange hair. Limps. Carries broad-axe."

It was as if someone unseen had slapped Caderyn. He flopped back into his chair, rubbed his face, grimaced due to the sickening wave that washed over him. "Verum," he uttered. "The gods have no mercy. Judoc..." What apology could make up for his cruelty?

"I should not a take coin," Judoc repeated, rocking. "Should not yet could not help. Tired of work. Of sea. Fish-smell. Should not a take coin but no hope ever have something otherwise. Just wanted..." Teardrops joined his beads of sweat. "Poor girl. Pretty girl."

Jana, crying, slipped outside.

Judoc hiccupped. "I watch them carry poor pretty girl. Lil' sack. She wake though. Poor pretty thing. She look me. Made me rotten fruit inside. Coward. Could not stop plagiariae. Did not try. So I keep coin Praedator give. I want be happy, have home, warm bed. Soft bed. Away from stink. Nice place. Find girl me. If can forget, forgive coward me. Should not a take coin. Nulla. Gods punish me. You evil man mean like hunter. Nasty, foul. Whole world."

Caderyn rose on knocking knees. "I..." A sorry still evaded him. He gripped the back of his chair, hung his head, heard a boy's helpless pleas, memory-felt the bush leaves brushing him as he wept. "Where...? Where did Praedator...?"

"Boat. To scary piece land. No one live there. Bloody past. Sangin."

"San..." His stomach balled into a knot. What made him any better than the soldiers who raped the boy? He, now brother to them, tortured the innocent. "Do you mean Sanguinem Insula?"

Snuffling, nodding, Judoc murmured, "Isle of blood."

"Apol—" Useless to say. Useless to try. Caderyn stumbled outside to lean over the bannister and suck in air until his gut ceased attempting to void itself.

Jana stroked his arm. "I, too, thought Judoc was lying."

He straightened and wiped away saliva. "I should have given Acteon's description rather than his name. Stupid. I broke that wretch's finger for no reason. All he wanted was to escape the muck of his life. What he got was injury and shame, this when he has tormented himself and is incapable of living with what he has done. How does he differ from me? Or I from Acteon or the soldiers, harming others for my own gain and pleasure?"

"You did what you did because a girl's life is in the balance."

As was sixty thousand chrysae. Which more concerned him he was unsure. Or maybe he did know and pretended otherwise. His lips, oh how he wanted to wipe them, stretch them. He instead pulled Jana to him. "What I said in the plaustrum."

"You long for drink?"

"Not yet." Caderyn gazed into her bloodshot eyes beset in shining jade. "Because of you."

XXI

SEVERUS

No drawn-out, patient strokes this time to how he made love to Jana. Caderyn—on bended knees, lightheaded, chest aflame, and hips weakening—hammered into her, pulse throbbing in his temples due to his exertions quickening because Jana had never looked more erotic than she did before him on all-fours. Her slender waist passed between his hands to a well-defined torso that sloped to shoulders broad for a woman's though not so wide and indelicate they were masculine. She held up her head, neck twisted. Her expression—eyelids lowered to slits and mouth gaping open—was of a lover lost in pleasure.

"Eleison," she urged, gasping. "Finish."

He yearned to, *ached* to, but whenever he neared release, the release spurned him, withering at the memory-sound of Judoc shrieking. Why, Caderyn kept thinking at the most inopportune moment, should he feel this good considering what he had done? Shutting his eyes, believing that might allow him to concentrate on the now, was a mistake. Blindness further opened the door to the past, so he marveled at the sweat beading and streaming on Jana's back, her writhing muscles, and sensational natis. Lantern-light coming in the window fell just right, blessing him with glimpses of his glistening cock slipping in and out of her.

He rammed faster, harder.

The rectangular bed—a new style borrowed from a foreign land—shimmied, headboard thumped. What had been moans of pleasure coming from her turned into whimpers. Even still, despite the quivering of her limbs that made Caderyn wonder how much longer she could last, she leaned forward upon his pulling away and rammed backward as he went into her.

"Mictus," she begged, pleading for him to spill his seed. "Mictus. Eleison. Mictus."

He tried, oh how he tried. The pressure in his testicles was crippling, like seconds after someone had kicked him there. If she...as if reading his mind, she groped back and between her legs to fondle his groin, her fingernails teasing him. The orgasm was not the tidal wave he needed or expected, not even a trickle but a mere dab, his bellowing more from frustration than gratification. He collapsed to the side and rolled onto his back.

Jana laid beside him and put her head on his shoulder as she flopped her arm around his midsection. The leg she flung across his thighs almost bumped his erection.

"Whew," she whispered.

Caderyn kissed her on the forehead, whispered for her to rest. "Somnus, mea dulcis."

A few minutes later she snored. He doubted whether the inn crumbling around them could awaken her. The thought brought a smile, his first since Judoc; debauched behavior in a new place. So much for the fresh beginning and not wanting—

Caderyn raised his head, rammed the back of it hard on the foreign-styled rectangular pillow too soft for his liking, too different than the bound rolls of cloth used with a domestic bed. The innkeeper boasting the Taurus Exsecti was the singular inn within Permia renting beds capable of sleeping four grew perturbed when Caderyn had asked why nothing changed for the better. If Calasade was to be influenced by foreign lands, why not with—No, again he refused to think of *that*, and glared at the rafters where a yellowish glow illuminated them, hoping to grow bored and for his mind to tire, that he get rest for tomorrow, a busy day.

He slid from under Jana and slunk towards the window. Another thing he abhorred regarding foreign influence was the flooring. Wood no matter how smoothed was rough against bare feet as opposed to marble. When he got to the window, instead of closing the shutters, he looked below onto the terrace, staying to the side so he was invisible to the party drinking at a table. He checked the garden's darkened corners and beneath the stairs granting boarders access to their rooms. His gaze traced the garden-walls. Atop them sat lion statues posed to attack. With the walls extending to the inn's third floor there was little need to worry over enemies scaling—

From where had that thought come?

He flicked his middle-finger against his thumb.

A nice spot the garden. From its elms hung tied curry and primulae in pots, the combined scents of spiciness and flowers the lone pleasing aspect regarding his and Jana sitting with Mathis and Jacob while the four of them debated strategy.

Jacob. "Our problem is reaching Sanguinem Insula in secrecy. The sea is visible in every direction from that old fortress tower, even at night. We could wait for clouds to block the astrum, but what then?"

Caderyn nodded not in agreement with what he expected Jacob to next state but in contemplation of a smarter idea.

The big man snorted. "Idiots us, were we to try mooring at a cliff at night, especially in rough water. You can be sure Acteon watches the one beach. Us shoring there would turn us into porcae ripe for the slaughter." His stare drifted from the pile of plates containing remnants of their dinner to rest on Caderyn. "Your resolve should not have mirrored an old man's verpus. So you broke a finger. What of it? Me, I say we revisit this Judoc, and force greater detail."

"You," Caderyn grumbled, "are cruel."

"Better callous than ignorance and us gathering as many warriors as we can from who knows where and storming that island."

"We do that, it will not surprise me to find Indrasena dead and Acteon gone. He will have an escape ready. Shrewd as he is, he will dupe those with him to fight us while he vanishes."

"You men." Jana chuckled but without humor. "So assumptive and trusting of scant promise. All Judoc said was where Acteon took Indrasena. Beyond this we have naught. Who among us can swear to Acteon and Indrasena remaining on Sanguinem?"

Caderyn gulped the last of his water. "A fine point. The crux is determining that without endangering the girl. Any ideas?"

At that she shrugged.

Mathis. "I am the cleptus among us. Leave sneaking onto the isle and scouting to me. I will find out if they are there and from that we can plan."

"Oh?" Jacob sniggered. "How are you to perform this magical feat?"

"On the morrow we get Lepidus to hire a piscator to pretend to fish while he delivers me close to the island. Such a craft within the isle's vicinity will circumvent raising suspicions. Once the proconsul does this, we collect ocean debris—seaweed, reeds, planks, things that will float. We put that together, make it look natural. The piscator and I set sail. When the boat gets me near and the evening is dark enough, I drop in the water under the seaweed and reeds, direct it towards the beach. I will take a look around and swim back the following night. No one on the isle will be the wiser. Just make sure the fisherman intercepts me so I do not drown."

"And if the seas get rough," Jana said, "what then?"

"Mathis," —Caderyn set down his cup— "to do this is to put your life in danger for Indrasena, a woman you have never met."

"The same risk extends to each of us except Jana."

Caderyn flicked the cup's rim, wanting to get up, move, do *whatever*. "I will go."

"You are big and clumsy, easy to hear or spot."

"Still." He again flicked the cup's rim, creating tings with his fingernail.

Jana grabbed his hand. "Asinus."

Jacob. "Mathis and she are right. You go, you will get caught."

"So that is it? I am outvoted?"

They nodded one-by-one. Caderyn shoved back his chair in rising and dragged Jana up the stairs and into their room. That was when he tore off her clothing and attacked her in a fit of sexual fury from which his legs yet felt weak as he watched the party leave, wishing it was he and Jana.

Depart. How *tempting* that word. He rocked side-to-side to quell his urge to pace, to move, to—

Go. Do it. Wake her. Get out of here.

And leave for where?

Anyplace.

Why did he feel this way? Imagination—no, something was coming and nothing would be the same if he and Jana were here when it arrived. He perceived that no less than the uncomfortable floor his feet stomped across.

"Get up." He shook Jana. "Get up and get dressed."

"Wha…" She rose on an elbow, peeked through sleep-heavy eyelids.

"We need to leave. Now."

"Why? What is wrong?"

Caderyn rushed to his side of the bed. He plopped on the edge, grabbed his trousers, and thrust his legs in at the same time. "Something ill approaches." He yanked on his boots, did not bother with the straps, and reached for his vest, cursing his stupidity for leaving the mucrones at Lepidus's villa.

"Have you been drink—?"

"Not a drop. *Move now.*"

"How can you know—?"

"The war. Take each breath unaware which is your last, you get a sense for impending doom. Trouble nears, Jana. *Hurry.*"

Either she had adopted his paranoia or reacted to his tension; Caderyn heard her high-pitched groan and the blankets rustling as he slid an arm into his vest. Jana was pulling on her breeches, grousing over his acting a sex-craved fiend and tossing her clothes about the room, and demanding he help find her shoes. He glanced under the bed, across the room, atop and behind the clothing trunk. A sandal lay beneath the sheepskin-covered chair. He bolted there and got on a knee, groping under just as the door splintered and caved inward.

Several officers barged into the room, one barking, "Seize them!"

Caderyn grabbed the chair-legs, judging the furniture a formidable weapon given its heavy oak material. He waited until stomping neared then bounded and swept the chair side-to-side. The chair smashed the jaw of the first officer, carried on left-to-right. It hit the next diasostes wearing an identical open-faced helmet and mail shirt that jingled as the man went limp and dropped. Three additional diasostae came in a rush, charging Caderyn, and shoved him against the wall, rattling the window. The officer in the middle bombarded Caderyn's midsection with a volley of punches that cracked at least two of his ribs, sparking explosions of inferno and agony, similar to but many times worse than the nastiest side-cramp he had gotten running for miles when his unit was in full retreat.

He doubled over, spit draining out his mouth.

Someone grabbed his hair and slammed his head against the wall. His vision dimmed. Jana's screaming gained a distant, tunnel resonance. Caderyn blinked his eyes, willed them to stay open, for the blurriness to go away as he watched Jana struggle to get free of an officer's arms crushing her bare midriff.

A chuckle bitter and low came from the doorway. Lepidus. Dressed in his finest stola and mantle, he marched into the room, chin held high. On his mantle hung the sun emblem he donned when tending to official business.

He pointed a trembling finger at Caderyn. "You wanted to meet the commander of Floridus's policemen. There he is. The man who pummeled you. Atilius."

"What..." Caderyn huffed, wincing from his attempts to breathe. Were it not for the pain rippling along his ribcage and spearing his lungs, he would have believed this a nightmare. What was transpiring contained an overwhelming sensation of the surreal that had interrupted a dream in which everything had been if not perfect then pleasant in comparison.

Lepidus came on in measured steps, making and unmaking fists. "The speculator you chased was mine. I arranged for him after you returned from the lake." He gestured at Jana. "*Insipid* woman. Her tantrum affirmed my suspicions." The proconsul reared back his hand. For a moment the hand stayed aloft, trembling like the finger Lepidus had pointed, then shot forward, its palm smacking Caderyn's cheek. "My man informed me of what he overheard at the dock. From Judoc I learned Indrasena's location. Your" —he jabbed Caderyn's chest— "services are unwanted *and* unneeded. Atilius and his men will rescue Indrasena."

"Lepidus!" Jana beat against the arms squeezing her.

The proconsul turned long enough to screech, "Shut up. You shut up or I will bash your face." He resettled his glower on Caderyn. "Insect I will squash under my heel, you and that *putida*—my fetid slut for a wife—you two are under arrest for Adulteriis Coercendis." Lepidus wiped the back of his wrist across his mouth and smiled a venom-laced grin. "The crime of a plebs fornicating with the spouse of a nobilis is punishable by death. For both parties."

Caderyn lunged forward, his assault halted by war-hammer clouts to his face. He must have blacked out.

When he came-to, Lepidus was standing in front of Jana and spat each word. "No trial. No need. None. Witnesses. Servae, speculator, the cupo of this hospitium, these diasostae. Evidence. Your breasts. Suck-marks on them. That mussed bed. Semen the medicus will collect upon scraping your theca."

"You do not dare," Jana shrilled.

"I do, if for no other reason than to have one last sight at the thing that caused your downfall, then—" He sliced his hand through the air.

Her face whitened. "You *cannot*."

Lepidus's laugh reoccurred, this time heartless enough to cause goose-bumps. "Do not think the Lux Latum can save you. Oh, there may be an initial resistance to my enforcing such an archaic law, but said law will be enforced."

"What" —Caderyn gasped— "do you mean?"

The proconsul whirled. "The medicus will remove Jana's labia, as any unfaithful mongrel-bitch deserves. After that she is to spend her life isolated. How many her remaining days total depends on you. You, Fortis, will fight for my ludus upon the Bleeding Grounds of Floridus. I told you during our meeting at the Twisted Vine you would one day yelp at the end of my leash."

Caderyn bellowed. He bellowed until tears came and his roaring died because Atilius had throttled him.

Lepidus smirked. "Should you lose and I suspect it was on purpose, consider Jana's life forfeit, she condemned to die on the Bleeding Grounds with you watching. Your life, however..." The proconsul strolled over and patted Caderyn on the cheek. "No game's editor is to ever call for your demise nor an opponent slay you. Rest assured you will subsist tortured by guilt knowing your actions resulted in the deaths of *two* women."

XXII

TRAGOEDIA

The amber orb was a product of her imagination. Indrasena had come to understand this while healing inside the tent and attempting to communicate with the bimembrae, came to understand although the beasts could sense her they were not connected to her as she to them. Thus her control over them was never to be absolute.

Control...?

Influence fit better, she decided, staring at the bimembri heart set atop a pedestal within the fortress's inner-bailey. The pedestal missing its bust stood half in the shadow of parapets not laying in crumbled heaps. The heart measured smaller than those Saeva had tossed inside her pit-prison and came from a pregnant bimembra gray-skins insisted fight a bimembrus.

She blinked against welling tears then saw vermes slithering across the piece of meat—all it was, just a piece of meat, not the sentient beings she held precious. Another blink and the vermes vanished, the illusion brought on from the worms and hearts being forever linked in her mind. She kept staring not to see if the vermes might reappear or because looking caused her no torment, but because hallucinations and recalling the nightmare of a vermisi assault were a marked improvement over peering inside the fighting-pit a few strides off. Long gone were the spiked poles jutting from the arena's sides, pilfered for reuse or rotted to nothing after undergoing harsh seasons as recent as countless generations, their nonexistence leaving behind gaping holes and depressions in the pit's walls.

How ancient the dungeon in which Saeva imprisoned her and her familia in separate cells; from where, once per day, a Saevum led them into sunlight one at a time to check on their conditions, ensure each recovered from snakebites and had not suffered additional puncture-wounds, be they serpent or insect.

A dangerous place the decomposing fortress—yes, decomposing—the place seemed *alive* with remnants of horrors— wherein she had spotted amazing things while getting herded from the dark to the light, among them a skull similar in shape to a dog's but twice her height. In glimpsing an armory she expected the rusted swords and axes, the cobweb-covered shields. What surprised her—no, shocked—were the throat-harnesses able to encircle a horse's midsection. Pater said the wearers of these were dracones, winged monsters unseen since the Great Confrontation started through the godlike power of the castle's overlord, a Saevum who ruled dracones along with numerous other beasts, including bimembrae.

Regnorum ancestors had named him Bestialis.

Sometimes late at night she laid awake listening to creepy-crawly things ticking their ways along the floor, walls, and ceiling, fearing Bestialis's haunting presence in the second she went from sweating to shivering, during those minutes her outward breaths clouded in the moonlight glowing through holes too high for her to reach, squeeze through, and escape. Not that escaping ranked among her immediate aspirations nowadays. Not without taking Pater and Mater embracing each other opposite her across the fighting-pit and her brother. He wept inside the pit, petrified of the bimembrus fifty paces away, of it attacking—as a Saevum ordered her to command the animal.

If she rebuked...

Indrasena raised her gaze from the heart to Hunter-Man. "Their threat is real?"

"Verum."

...the Saevi leader swore through the sketches on a wax tablet to ravage Mater unto death, force her husband and children to watch.

Indrasena was not curious and neither did she care about the hunter's reply, but she needed to stall. "Did you know your partners to be capable of such cruelty?"

"Nulla."

As when smiling, his troubled frown was one-sided. Gray-skins named him Praedator, but should have called him Bifax—two-faced. Mean-spirited of her to think of him that way, yes, seeing how he snuck her and her familia extra food, but the moniker fit given he betrayed his country and was doing the same to those with whom he aligned after gleaning they might turn on him. Despicable. Though if made to state truths, she must admit she lacked the blind hatred to blame him as much as she wanted. Saeva had put Hunter-Man/Praedator/Acteon/Bifax in the impossible position of choosing between homeland and wife. No one among those Indrasena considered acquaintance or dear would have sided different, including her father.

"Puella," Hunter-Man said. Sadness, or at least a convincing manifestation of the emotion, inundated his gruff tone.

Puella. The nickname he had given her when she was a child held various meanings in Regni patois depending on the context, any save one a term of endearment. Daughter, maiden, slavegirl, sweetheart, young woman, or wife. Of those, did he refer to her as maiden or serva?

Sweetheart?

Perhaps. They had developed an uncomfortable friendship after he expressed his regret beyond counting over what he and Saeva had done on those occasions he snuck the food. Often he ruminated on days of old, of his and her playing games prior to his lighting out.

Ever the hunter him.

His large hand fell soft on her shoulder. "Puella, them not wait long. Must decide."

She meant to lower her head a little for relooking at the heart, but with strength abandoning her, Indrasena's chin bumped her collarbone. "How can I choose between the two of them? Mater, frater."

"Me, you have one way out."

Try as she might to hold the tears, one leaked from her, spoiling her pledge to not again cry, for the world was ugly and her blubbering prettified nothing. "You will help?"

"Aio." His sigh warmed the back of her neck. "If me know what happened after Saeva give wax tablet, me mayhap choose dead. Should not a married wife, but man ugly as me get lonesome. Me get feeling no gold or ship. Saeva hate Regna, even me."

She peeked at the gray-skins scattered within the inner-bailey, the majority by her parents, and counted twenty. "Their number on Sanguinem."

"Thirty."

"Can you free the bimembrae?"

"Me slow, limp. Loose one afore draw attention."

"If—" She caught herself gesturing before anyone noticed. "In the pit, were my familiare to climb out and attack...?"

"Rest gray-skins come running, help brothers. Me free every beast."

Seven bimembrae lived after the massacres for their hearts and her influencing two—*nulla*. She shunned the memory of earlier that morning. "Can my familiaria defeat the Saeva?"

"Me not know."

She shook her head. "To sway so many at once."

"Beast help own kind, too. No need to control."

"But if I fail to stop the bimembrae after the gray-skins…" She pictured the bodies of her familia getting torn asunder as a result of her brashness and wiped the streams from her cheeks.

"Fret naught. You eyne. Where dots then spots now be circles. Hard to make beast fight each other. You did. Heart on stone proof."

The survivor of that battle stood in the pit as terrified as her brother and whimpered in a way that ached her bones. Could the bimembrus fight long enough for others to join the fray, assuming she possessed the callousness to persuade it?

She bit her bottom lip, issued a silent prayer to Fatum. "Will you betray me?" Stupid question since what deviator replied yes.

His grip tightened on her shoulder.

Indrasena took a deep breath to rein in the twitchiness of her gut. "Sneak away once my familiare growls and paws at the dirt, when he has captured Saevi attention. Break the head off a spear and use the handle to unlatch cage-doors from a distance. Let my familiaria come out on their own. Know you will die should you prod them, keep the spearhead, or go armed. Neither look them in the eyne. They take that for aggression. Kneel, stare at the ground if any approach you. Beseech the gods."

She shuffled her feet in turning, took baby-steps to the edge of the fighting-pit, and made eye-contact with her brother, tried to impart reassurance. Some lies, even silent ones, served a good purpose. This she had come to understand, too, not on her own but courtesy of Hunter-Man.

As she inched her gaze to the bimembrus, her familiare's whining changed to a howl. Indrasena folded her hands into fists.

Her back straightened, shoulders squared. She shut her eyes and took drawn-out, controlled breaths while picturing the beast's three straight and cone-shaped horns, the protruding brow, orange irises, jowls, where he bled out his hairless and brown gargantuan muscular body. She envisioned mending his gashes, kissing them.

The loving mother.

White particles materialized in the darkness of her mind, floated to the middle of her forehead, and melded. The fuzzy dot expanded, smoothened. She breathed calm into the circle, requested it flatten and elongate to a thread, angle towards her nose and seep out her nostril. Free, comparable to a feather, the thread languished side-to-side on the breath she blew that took the thread halfway across the pit. There the thread drifted to the bimembrus glaring upward, wafted past his bestial teeth and entered his crimson gullet, sank in the bubbling fluid of a stomach digesting pieces of Scar-face, the plagiarius who had abused her.

Her bimembrus—a champion of the fighting-pit twice this day—quieted its howl. The tipping-point had arrived when the familiare denied or did as she bade.

Sense her desires. Commit acts she imagined herself doing.

"Sentis cogitationibus mies," Indrasena hissed. *"Facere ut opinor."*

Praedator moved into the shadow of the parapets, waited until the beast in the fighting-pit roared and stomped and Indrasena's poor frater shrieked, startling birds from trees and enticing Saeva to dare the pit's edge for a better view. He slunk to where time had reduced a great wall to rubble and turned for a look at the girl now a young woman. Difficult for him to consider her as such, but there she was, womanhood obvious in her curves, most of them uncovered with her donning just the leather straps that draped to her knees.

Her getting even that tiniest bit of clothing proved an ordeal, the memory of it causing him to chuckle as he pictured the expression of the Saevum leader upon comprehending her sketch. The loincloth the leader recognized, but the etching of the strophium baffled him. In Saevi culture breasts were venerated, to be exposed for they symbolized motherhood and power. Besides bewilderment, awe laced the leader's mien. For Indrasena to make any demands given her predicament, her life and those of her family in the hands of the person she confronted...No, Praedator thought, she was not anymore a clumsy, lanky thing but a *woman* possessing fortitude unlike any he had seen. She would never have traded her homeland for love or coin. Bravery in the face of fear, intelligent and wise regardless age, moral turpitude without the inclination to judge, stoic yet impassioned; these were the qualities of leaders who inspired others to risk their lives, *others* being those sharing her admirable characteristics and them yearning to make amends for missteps spurred by personal shortcomings.

He nodded as if confirming to himself his intentions and lumbered along a path Saeva from a bygone era carved into the mountain. The farther he descended, the taller the cliffs loomed at either side, dwarfing him. He passed under a wooden arch that had withered but somehow persisted, as if its original architect defied the ages themselves even while dead. Praedator's wife claimed the arch eons ago presented Bestialis's name in white paint on crimson-colored stain. He adopted this island as home, a sanctuary away from those he wished to protect should things go awry when practicing his magic.

Up top, within the fortress laboratory, he learned secrets kept by the gods. Here at the base of the path where Praedator caught his breath and rested his throbbing ankle Bestialis died, a sword through his chest pinning him to the ground while a Unayelum lopped off his head. Easy to see the spot. The dirt colored darker.

Praedator shook off the chills traversing his spine and continued on around the bend, sidestepping Saeva charging up the path to aid their shouting brothers and sisters, then headed towards the line of unattended campfires and populated cages. Rather than liberate the beasts, he went inside the tent and fetched a pair of oars leaning in the corner.

Back outside he bypassed the fires, the cages—imprisoned bimembrae howled upon him limp-hurrying past, incensed or alarmed by his broad-axe—and followed the trail letting out on the beach.

Across the beach and propped against a boulder awaited the boat, his salvation, the tender used in getting to-and-fro the main ship not scheduled to return until the next full moon. No witnesses then to raise an alarm over his escaping. Yes, he would have to row for miles across an ocean that could turn nasty at any moment, but his chances of survival improved a hundredfold doing that than rebelling alongside the girl and her pets. He felt awful, having duped Indrasena into thinking he joined her plight, but contriteness—when you got to the heart of things—was not worth dying for.

The trout swimming a familiar stream dividing into two did not go to the rivulet ending in a waterfall.

He stepped from good, solid ground to the sound of Indrasena's oft-repeated scream—this one from heartbreak, frustration, or terror?—and onto the beach. Mobility was always challenging even in the best of circumstances, but nigh impossible on sand where wise seafarers ran instead of walked because running eased crossing that which gave way. With his ankle, though, and him hitch-hustling, that leg was like a stake driven into mud.

Push, step, pull, huff.

A quarter across the godforsaken beach his chest verged on collapsing. Halfway his lower body numbed except for his hips burning in red-hot agony. Three-fourths to the tender he heard Saevorum cursing and arrows in flight.

Humming, whirring, sticking the sand inches from him in quiet *thew, thew, thews.*

Praedator tried to dodge and stumbled, had to drop his broad-axe to keep from falling. Onward he limped.

Push, step, pullhuff. Push, steppullhuff. Pushsteppullhuff.

Thunk. Thunk-thunk-thunk.

Arrows which passed so close he could feel the air from them quivered along the side of the boat. He dropped the oars, went to grab the trim and roll over the tender when something pinched his shoulder, twisted and flung him to the sand.

Then the real pain started.

XXIII

EPIL⊙GUS

Intermittent holes in the tunnel allowed intense beams of concentrated light that did little to illuminate the areas in between and bends often went full-dark. Sconces hung on the walls, but no one had lit the oil in the saucers and for that Caderyn was glad. He did not need the stink of burning fuel to mingle with the sweat of the harenarae caged two or three to a cell awaiting their turns to fight, perhaps die; their collective mood somber. If not for those boasting of prowess and others howling, the tunnel of Floridus's Bleeding Grounds mimicked a tomb. In occasional moments of quiet that prevailed upon a guard shouting out someone's name, like what happened when the custos hollered "Thalazar", the terrified uttered their desperate prayers as if the gods might answer and cease this madness.

The young man sharing Caderyn's chamber yawned, exited the cell, and stretched. Black hair dropped midway along his back ridged in muscles.

"May Alea grant you success," Caderyn said.

Thalazar dropped his arms and peered over his shoulder. "Alea? That putida can choke on my verpus. Fatum, too, should I fall. God of fate. What shit." He smiled crookedly. "Until I return either drunk on blood or a lifeless husk."

The custos shut the grated door, muttered about craziness as he led the man off and Caderyn leaned against the wall no one had bothered covering with limestone, wishing he were as nonchalant regarding life and death. Of the hundred combatants in this tunnel he guessed his cellmate was the sole fighter zealous for battle.

Thalazar. Odd name. Exotic. Foreign. And false given he spoke with the sharpness of those from Elasai, their accent stressing consonants. How he got this far north and what led to his enslavement as a harenarius were mysteries since the man rebuffed any subject of importance. A criminal—at least Caderyn suspected as much though remained bewildered over why Thalazar bore no facial brand. Were they both to survive this day, Caderyn weighed prying, opted for letting the questions go unanswered and save these inconsequential matters for pondering.

Those kept his mind off *her*.

Some.

From outside the tunnel boomed the announcing of Thalazar and his opponent. With butterflies flitting in his gut Caderyn closed his eyes and left them that way until scraping footsteps neared. Custodes wore boots. Servae and harenarae went barefoot.

Nobilia donned sandals.

Lepidus stopped in front of the cell, an undoubtable attempt to show how brave he was strolling alone the tunnel populated by vipers. The proconsul raised the lantern he carried. Wrinkles around his eyes had deepened since they last saw each other.

"Three years," said Lepidus. "A long time to wonder if we found Indrasena and whether Jana lives. She does. Look for her at the podium to stand and wave. You may even hear her call your name when you step upon the sands. This she will do every time you battle. This she will do upon my order, good little lapdog the mongrel-bitch is nowadays."

Caderyn bit his tongue and resumed staring down the tunnel, determined to give the proconsul no satisfaction from needling him.

Lepidus hummed a short, happy tune. "I reconsidered my decision of isolating her. Better motivation for you that during your fights you see Jana draws breath. In this way you will keep wanting to do the same. Sweeter for me, too, you knowing she fulfills my every whim while you tussle with this life you detest."

Caderyn kept his expression blank and listened to swords clanging.

"Silens? Verum? I hoped for you to yelp. But" —Lepidus sighed— "dogs care for so little. I see your same dead-eyed look in Jana when I mount her. Me, I am not so devoid of feeling; fact is compassion compelled me here so I could tell you what happened to Indrasena. See how benevolent I am?"

The fist Caderyn concealed behind his thigh strained his fingers and knuckles.

Lepidus clucked his tongue. "When the vigilum and his men reached Sanguinem Insula, they found naught on the island. Well, this is not absolute truth. There were deep holes and evidence of a large camp. I at first suspected upon hearing this that your allegiance changed afore your arrest and you warned Acteon through a messenger." The proconsul chuckled. "That is, I thought this until Atilius reported what else they discovered."

I do not care. Thinking the lie kept Caderyn from stating it.

"Not curious? I will say nonetheless. They found this *thing* shackled in a pit. Beg for scraps and I shall tell you its name."

The crowd roared, signifying Thalazar's fight was over. Caderyn prayed his own followed and was as brief however it ended.

Lepidus harrumphed. "A mongrel starves without its treats. Why delay your entreaty? Come on, pup. Yelp for me."

He looked up then. And offered his biggest grin.

As the crowd went wild and the main gate of the tunnel thereafter rattled open, the proconsul's eyes grew wide. He spoke faster than before. "This *thing* the vigilum found was Acteon. He rambled of traitorous gray-skins and how his Saevi wife was an ingrate whore. His lies could not save him. These past three years Acteon has spent in a dungeon awaiting his execution."

The clinking of boots drew closer. Infectious guffaws echoed at the nearest curve.

"Aio," crowed Thalazar. "I showed Fatum."

The proconsul gawked in that direction. "You are to slay Acteon for treason during intermission—"

"LEPIDUS!"

Caderyn saw Thalazar at the tunnel's curve shoving a custos prior to getting dragged beyond sight. An unseen scuffle ensued—cursing, punches landing on flesh and others on metal, armor clanging against stone. Lepidus whined and fled from the melee. Thalazar sprinted past, face set in marked determination, silence, then grunting followed by the proconsul screaming for help. He must have gotten it. There were shouts. Additional sounds of fighting. Minutes later two custodes hauled an unconscious Thalazar back to Caderyn's cell. A nasty bruise bubbled his oozing forehead. The crazy bastard was grinning.

"You, Fortis." The custos pointed. "Be better behaved than him. Come."

Caderyn rose and entered the tunnel that seemed to move, was a snake slithering. Vertigo. He put a hand on the guard's shoulder to brace himself.

"Are you ill?" the custos asked.

He opened his mouth to answer and shut it, swallowed something bitter and burning.

The custodes herded him into a small room. He assumed it was where the medicus tended to the injured until spotting the armor on the table. Those pieces the guards picked up and put on him. A lorica robusta—back and front smelted for a muscular torso—was decorated with yellow tribal designs outlined in orange, jagged except where the lines curved inward to form axe-blades meeting in the center of his chest. Spaulders for protecting his shoulders and a codpiece were modeled in the shape of skulls; so, too, the ridged helmet they fashioned to his head that ruined his peripheral vision and greaves to guard his shins. None of it a custom fit. The armor styled after Mors—the god of death—was loose in places, tight in others.

"Mucrones?" Caderyn muttered.

"At the portcullis," replied a custos. "Handed to you upon your introduction."

A wise idea, leaving him unarmed until necessary.

Several guards wielding long pole-axes—securis destructivae—stood along the ramp leading to the portcullis accessing the Bleeding Grounds. As Caderyn waited in front of the gate, he concentrated on nothing in particular, looking at how bright the sand was, listening to crowd murmurs while ignoring all Lepidus had said and trying to not consider Jana, how he missed her, what she must be going through.

Now was not the time for such things. He did, however, reflect on Acteon and what it meant to kill a person once considered a friend.

The announcer's voice boomed loud and rich.

"Citizens of Calasade, it is mid-day and it is *hot*. Yet our discomfort from this scorching summer is naught as we have witnessed many fine contests from the lower rungs of harenarae on this inauguration of the greatest amphitheatrum Fors has hitherto seen. A pleasing enough beginning, verum, but I am glad to shout out to you now the time has come for *superior* entertainment."

The crowed whooped and stomped. Dust cascaded from the ceiling above Caderyn.

"Because Clupeus," the announcer hollered, "has smiled upon us with too much warmth, let us beseech Pluvia for rain. Let us have said rain by way of torrential blood to be spilled from those who dared insult our great nation with their criminality. On this day...

"ON...THIS...DAY

"...we have *ten* murderers, *five* rapists, and a *single* plagiarius you will see die first."

Long seconds passed while the crowd applauded.

"We shall witness these societal defects tremble, hear their cries for mercy ungiven. We will *rejoice* at their whimpers and *revel*—aio, REVEL—in their pathetic pleas as they DIE at the hands of...

"...

"*MORS!*"

"Your cue," said the custos holding out a pair of mucrones.

Caderyn took the weapons and gripped their hilts. Chains rattled. The portcullis rose. He ducked and went under, stepping from the tunnel's dankness into the freshness of open air and onto the sands, his jaw dropping over the crowd dizzying in its mass. The mural at Lepidus's villa had given him an idea of the Bleeding Grounds' sheer size, but that idea was a gross injustice. He turned around slow, going full-circle and taking in the expanse of a hundred yards in length and seventy-five in width. Everywhere he looked people leapt and pumped their hands. Despite having promised himself to not enthrall the masses, he thrust his swords overhead.

"Mors!" the crowd chanted.

Goose-bumps riddling his skin, he strode to the center of the Bleeding Grounds. No sooner had the chills left him than they returned as the portcullis rose at the opposite end of the Bleeding Grounds.

Caderyn stabbed his mucrones into the sand-covered dirt and fumbled with the ties on the back of his helmet. To burgeoning cheers he loosened the straps and threw the helmet as far as he could, just missing the first row of people. The helmet ricocheted off the wall inches taller than the referee who gestured at the piece of armor then at the people behind him.

"Aio," Caderyn shouted.

Roars of approval reached an apex once the referee tossed the helmet that flipped over and over, reflecting sunlight until vanishing amid a sea of hands.

Seconds later the throngs booed. Caderyn turned towards Acteon approaching. The beast-hunter was thinner than before, a veritable lurching skeleton wearing a subligaculum and carrying a single weapon, his broad-axe.

Identical to every criminal except escaped slaves brought to the sands for justice, Acteon had a final chance at surviving. To win—as Thalazar had done against three harenarae in a lesser arena—was to keep fighting. Not freedom by any means yet an improvement over death.

Partial improvement.

The beast-hunter halted ten paces away. "Years it be. Still no drink?"

"None to be had within the harenari prison-city." Caderyn bobbed his weapons, appreciating their lightness. "Why did you take the girl?"

"Coin. Trust no gray-skin. Look where me stand after me marry one. On sands."

"Saeva forced you to take Indrasena?"

Acteon shook his head. His hair greasy and dirty hardly moved from his shoulders. "Hire me to find magum bestiae. Me, others take girl to isle to train bimembrae. She magi. Yellow dots, bigger spots, circles. Gray-skins blame me for girl and beast fighting them. They go, take girl. Leave me in pit."

"What fate befell your wife?"

"Me not know or care."

"Why did Saeva want Indrasena to train the bimembrae?"

"Why you think? Another Great Confrontation coming. Lepidus think me lie. He say partners sell Indrasena to other ludus, but girl in Avia now. Calasade five, ten years peace mayhap but that no concern me any."

Crowd members stomping their feet at first imitated distant knocking, but the clamor soon matched the noise of ground rumbling. Whoever the architect, they did an amazing job with acoustics. Every sound magnified, including the roar Acteon let loose.

The masses hoorayed as the beast-hunter rushed and Caderyn stood unmoving.

Waiting.

For Acteon's wheezing to louden. Then he sidestepped and stuck out his foot. The beast-hunter tripped, his huge weapon careening him further off-balance.

The people had come for a show and Caderyn decided to let them have it. Twirling one sword after the other, he spun. Acteon acted the huffing bull preparing to charge and raised his axe, bellowed another battle-cry.

The beast-hunter charged.

Caderyn pitied the man. Their fighting-ability was equal before his training to become an harenarius, but now he possessed a cat's reflexes and ducked at the instant the beast-hunter swung his axe. When Caderyn sprang from his crouch, he rammed a bulbous mucronis hilt into Acteon's chin, shattering teeth and causing a trail of blood to spew out the beast-hunter's mouth. Caderyn whirled, raising his foot and driving it into Acteon's gut in the manner Thalazar had schooled him. The beast-hunter doubled over, stumbled.

To the crowd's thunderous applause Caderyn tossed aside one of his blades, lifted its twin high. He strode to Acteon kneeling and gasping and rammed a knee into the beast-hunter's face, knocking him over. Crimson-colored spittle bubbled from between his lips. His gut rose and fell with each labored breath taken. He moaned as the tip of Caderyn's sword pricked that soft bit of flesh preceding his sternum.

"Kill!" the crowd demanded. "*Kill!*"

Whatever callousness keeping the woman he loved alive demanded, regardless the repulsiveness the promise of vengeance stipulated, Caderyn would commit either without hesitation.

He pushed his blade into and through Acteon's vital organs, numb to the screams and pleas to an uncaring god. After the words faded and Acteon gurgled no more, Caderyn backed off his friend's corpse. He strolled the way he had entered, towards the podium Lepidus and other nobilia occupied, where *she* stood dressed in a gray stola typical of slaves, palms covering her face, her shoulders bobbing as she wept.

"Jana," he yelled, staying outside the podium's shadow so she could better see him.

She lowered her hands, rested her fingers on the iron collar encircling her neck. A large bruise surrounded her nose crooked and flat, but the break had at least healed, unlike her swollen mouth and blackened right eye. Jana smiled how those mourning a spouse, parent, or child tried to show gratitude upon hearing condolences.

She was more beautiful than ever.

"Te amo," he said, choking off and refusing tears that arose from professing his love for her. "Upon a day—somehow, someway by the graces of the gods or not—I shall come for you. And him." Caderyn leveled his sword at Lepidus. "He will pay for what he has done tenfold."

JOIN MY STREET TEAM

What's a street team? A group of fans that support an author by getting the word out about the author's publications. This is done via social media platforms. Word-of-mouth (or media-of-mouth) is any author's greatest tool, especially in today's publishing world. Given the market is inundated with books on a daily basis, it's harder than ever for an author to get noticed. Without media/word-of-mouth, well, said author is about as dead in the water as a floating, bloated fish.

You're probably wondering what's in it for you. As a street team member you are first in line for advance reader copies and get sneak-peaks at upcoming publications. But that's not all. Members are eligible to win prizes from the promotions they join. Some of these prizes are amazing. How amazing? How about a First Edition Lord of the Rings trilogy? Others include free, signed Calasade paperbacks and gift cards from the store of their choice. Additional boons include participating in conversations with other fans, awarded swag (bookmarks, signed art, etc.), and personal interaction with Mark Stone. As if all the aforementioned isn't enough, members will receive exclusive autographed publications such as Calasade: Gilinard and Istel when the novella is complete. Shipped free of charge.

Register at authormarkstone.com to get in on a great opportunity!

LEAVE A REVIEW

MAKE A DIFFERENCE

There are trade-offs in publishing. For me, the trade-off came down to getting published by a big publisher or staying true to the vision of Calasade. I decided to stay true to the stories and the people in those stories despite my inability to compete with the big publishers regarding advertising. Reviews therefore are the single most important component for Calasade being successful.

So I need you, Dear Reader, in the worst way. Please leave a review on Amazon if you've liked what you read. Heck, even if you didn't. I strive to be the best writer I can. Any and all feedback will assist me in that.

Places to leave a review for this book by going to my Amazon page:

amazon.com/author/calasade

Thank you ever so much.

ABOUT MARK STONE

Mark Stone lives in Costa de Sol with his wife Cinta, his greatest inspiration. Having written award-winning Flash Fiction, he is now a novelist writing tales of Fantasy and Sword & Sorcery based in the Ancient Roman world of Calasade. When not writing, he's exploring ruins. When not writing or exploring ruins, he's at the beach.

Keep up with his publications at authormarkstone.com.

www.ingramcontent.com/pod-product-compliance
Lightning Source LLC
Chambersburg PA
CBHW051247250626
47155CB00009B/3205